The Memory
of Old Jack

WENDELL BERRY

*The Memory
of Old Jack*

COUNTERPOINT
BERKELEY

Library of Congress Cataloging-in-Publication Data
Berry, Wendell, 1934–
The memory of Old Jack / Wendell Berry.—1st Counterpoint pbk. ed.
p.   cm.

ISBN 13: 978-1-58243-043-0
ISBN 10: 1-58243-043-8
1. Port William (Ky. : Imaginary place) Fiction. 2. Aged men—
Kentucky Fiction. I. Title.
PS3552.E75M4   1999
813'.54—dc21   99–16086
                                            CIP

Book and jacket design by David Bullen Design

Printed in the United States of America

COUNTERPOINT
2560 Ninth Street
Suite 318
Berkeley, CA 94710
www.counterpointpress.com

30   29   28   27   26   25   24   23

I made this book
for my father,
its true source,
in gratitude
and in celebration

Author's Note

When I began to write about the people of the imagined community of Port William in 1955, I had no idea that I would still be writing about them in 1999. I had no plan, and I still don't.

Having had no plan, I have made "errors" of genealogy and geography that I haven't been aware of until readers (more alert and responsible than I am) have pointed them out to me.

In this new edition of *The Memory of Old Jack*, I have made some changes to correct those errors, and some changes merely to improve my editing.

Nothing of substance has been changed. Neither in this book nor in my thoughts have I qualified my loyalty to this old man and his hard-earned, beautiful knowledge.

One: Light

Since before sunup Old Jack has been standing at the edge of the hotel porch, gazing out into the empty street of the town of Port William, and now the sun has risen and covered him from head to foot with light. But not yet with warmth, and in spite of his heavy sheepskin coat he has grown cold. He pays that no mind. When he came out and stopped there at the top of the steps, mindful of the way the weight of his body is taking him, he propped it carefully with his cane and, in the way that has lately grown upon him, left it.

From the barn whose vaned cupola was visible over the house roof against the pale sky, Mat Feltner was calling his cows. Old Jack listened with an eagerness that carried him away from himself; for all his consciousness of where he was, he might have been asleep and dreaming. Mat waited, and called again. And then from the quieting of Mat's voice, Old Jack knew that the cows had come near and that Mat could see them moving up deliberative and shadowy out of the mists and the thinning darkness. And then he heard the barn doors slide open.

Except for the crowing now and then of roosters, the little town and its outskirts were quiet. Old Jack's mind was with Mat there in the barn, stirring about the lives of animals. He knew the solitude that Mat had entered at the beginning of every workday since his son was killed in the war. He knew the stiffness and pain that the tobacco cutting had placed

in Mat's back and shoulders and hands. He was aware of the deep som-
nolence of the hayricks in the loft of the barn.

The old man stood on the porch in the chill whitening of the dawn,
empty of himself as a public statue, while all in him that had kept most
alive lived in the waking barn with Mat. And he has continued to stand
there while the cries of roosters have flared and flared again across the
ridges, and the daylight and then the sunlight have come. He has heard
the waking of other farms, the summoning of stock from the pastures,
the occasional bawling of a cow. He has heard the tractors start, the wagons lumbering to the fields.

Though tractors draw them now, not horses and mules, the sound of
the wagons going out is the same as always. Now there is the alien commotion of iron and fire, but within it or under it there is the old rattling
and pounding of the empty wagon beds against the bolsters, hurrying
out over the rough farm roads in the cool of the morning. As he listened
there passed and passed again across the gaze of his memory a good
team of mules that he bought as three-year-olds from Graham Foresee
in the September of 1888.

They were a team of black, mealy-nosed mare mules with plenty of
size and depth of body, with a lot of lift in their motion, matched well
every way. Beck and Kate. As though the reins are in his hands and he
stands again on the rattling wagon, they are carrying him to the field.
The sun is just coming up. It is the fall of the year. The mules are in good
flesh, the hair glossy on them, and they are fresh from the night. They
step together in the harness with an eager lightness that for a moment
shortens his breath.

They were the first team of their quality that he ever owned. They
were, maybe, an extravagance. He bought them because he needed a
team, no question about that. But he bought as carefully as he did, and
paid the price he paid, in a kind of celebration of himself. He had owned
his place then—or owned the debt his father had left on it—for three
years. And though he had not yet cleared the farm of debt, he was clearing it. He was going to clear it. There was no longer any doubt in him
about his ability to do that. It had become plain to him that he was equal
to what would be required of him and to what he would require of
himself.

And so he bought the mules. He hunted until he found a pair that he could look at and use with the satisfaction of fulfilled judgment, and he paid what was necessary. He went on horseback to get them one Saturday evening after work, and led them home in the dark of the night. He missed a dance to go get them, and when something reminded him of it two or three days later he added that to the price.

The next day he could not stay away from the barn. He led the team out after breakfast and groomed them and stood them together in the barn lot. On his own ground they still looked well to him. They suited him.

In the afternoon he brought them out again and hitched them in the driveway of the barn and busied himself repairing and adjusting a set of harness for them. Though he is at the end now, looking back at the beginning, the pleasure of that work and what it anticipated comes to him again and fills his mind.

He is sitting in the doorway of the harness room, the wide front entrance of the barn standing open at his left so that he can look out across the barn lot at the back of the old house standing gray among its trees. His knife, a punch, and several thongs of rawhide lie on the bench beside him. A breeze draws through the driveway. Used as he is to the expansive labor of the fields, he is enjoying the smallness and neatness of this task.

He hears a horse's shod hoof strike rock and looks up to see Ben Feltner coming around the house on a gray mare; Mat, Ben's five-year-old son, is coming along behind him on a pony. Ben is married to Nancy, the only one of Jack's sisters who was still at home when he was born and who in the years after their mother died gave him most of his upbringing. It was Nancy who encouraged Jack to buy their home place, and Ben who went on his note at the bank. A large, gentle man with the beard and eyes of a patriarch though he is not yet fifty, Ben Feltner is a widely respected farmer and citizen. He has a provident, retentive mind, the exacting judgment of a stockman, a brief, dry wit.

If Nancy was Jack's mother after his real mother died when he was five, it could be said that both after and for a good many years before the death of his real father when Jack was eighteen, Ben stood before him as a father. That was never a declared relationship. Jack was too old and too proud by the time of his father's death to accept openly a paternal authority that he had not been born under, and Ben was not the sort to give advice that had not been asked for. But Ben was the man Jack watched and listened to and checked his judgment against. There were times when Jack would outline a problem, as if hypothetically, and Ben would say carefully what he thought "a fellow" ought to do in such a circumstance.

Since he signed Jack's note for the purchase of the farm, Ben has said simply nothing at all about it. The visits he has made to Jack's place have been casual, to the point of whatever business brought him, never taking him farther than the barn. But Jack has known that he has been watched, and he has had the feeling during the last several months that he is being watched with approval. All this is characteristic of Ben, who understands the enthusiasms that pertain to beginnings, and who has therefore, in his offhand way, deferred judgment for nearly three years.

For a while they pass the time of day there in front of the barn. Jack leads out the new team of mules, and they look at them and talk about them. But Ben does not get off his horse. He has come at last, Jack realizes, to see for himself. He was getting ready to go look up his stock, Jack says. Do they want to come along? He saddles his horse and they ride together, the two men followed by the boy on the pony, out the ridge behind the barn. Letting the horses loaf along through the bright, hot afternoon, they ride over all the fields, examining the condition of the ground, the crops, the pasture, the stock, the fences and buildings. Though Jack speaks of what he has done and is doing and what he hopes to do, Ben says little. Occasionally he asks a question or speaks to his mare or points something out to Mat. At times they ride along in silence. But Jack is aware that within the shadow of his hat brim Ben's eyes are seeing and considering everything.

They stop to let Mat have a swim in a little pool walled up in Jack's grandfather's time to catch the outflow of a spring. Jack and Ben hitch the horses and come and sit on the broad, moss-edged capstones of the wall in the shade of a huge sycamore. There comes upon them a deep pleasure in the leisurely afternoon. After Mat has dried himself in the sun and dressed and come to sit between them on the wall, they stay on, watching the little fish that live in the pool and the dragonflies that hover

over it. Outside the shade of the old tree the afternoon burns bright on the slopes of the pasture.

As the day cools toward sundown they ride back to the barn. Jack dismounts at the door and speaks a few jocular parting words to Mat. And then he turns to Ben, whose eyes—pleased, and in their distant way perhaps amused—are looking at him now. "Jack, my boy, you're doing all right." He touches the mare then and turns her, Mat following, and starts home. Jack watches them out of sight.

Though he stands leaning on his cane on the porch of the hotel in Port William, looking out into the first cool morning of September, 1952, he is not there. He is four miles and sixty-four years away, in the time when he had music in him and he was light. From the height of that time his mind comes down to him, a bird to the head of a statue, and another day of his old age lights the street. The chill has gone deep in him now. He will go down to Jasper Lathrop's store, where, though it is too early in the season yet to expect a fire, some of yesterday's warmth will have been held overnight. Smiting the edge of the porch sharply with his cane as if to set hard reality on the alert, taking careful sight on the stone steps, he lets himself heavily down.

Two : Ben

When Mat Feltner walked out into his front pasture in the course of his morning chores, he saw Old Jack standing on the hotel porch like the monument of some historical personage. It was still gray then, and he could only dimly make out the figure of the old man within the shadow of the porch roof.

Later, bringing the milk to the house, he looks again, and then he stands and looks, for Old Jack is still there as before, the dawn having come upon him.

Mat's grandson, Andy Catlett, who has been feeding and watering the hogs, comes quietly into the yard and stands beside him.

"How's the boy?" Mat says. And then, remembering that this is Andy's last day to be there—tomorrow he will be going away to school—Mat reaches his arm around the boy's shoulders and hugs him. They stand so for another moment, silently looking at Old Jack, who is looking away.

"Well," Mat says, as if to end a conversation of some length, "let's go eat breakfast."

They go in and strain the milk and wash, and come back to the kitchen. Sitting down at the table, Mat frowns and shakes his head.

"What's the matter?" Margaret asks.

Mat, who does not know that he has given any sign, looks up at his wife and smiles. "Nothing," he says. And then, knowing she will not believe that, he says, "Uncle Jack. He's been standing over there since before day-light. Just like he's bolted to the porch."

Margaret only nods. Mat lifts his coffee cup; she fills it and sits down.

Old Jack has become a worry to them. In the last several weeks his mind seems to have begun to fail. They have been watching him with some anxiety, they and the others of the community who care about him, for fear that in one of those spells when he seems to go away from himself he will fall and be hurt or will be hit by a car. They have all found him at the various stations of his rounds, just standing, as poignantly vacant as an empty house. And they have watched him, those who care about him, because they feel that he is going away from them, going into the past that now holds nearly all of him. And they yearn toward him, knowing that they will be changed when he is gone.

Mat suddenly laughs. "Burley Coulter was saying the other day that Uncle Jack's turning into a statue. That's going to be his metamorphosis. One day he'll just stop the way he does and never start again. The birds'll roost on him."

Margaret concedes a smile to Burley's fantasy. But she changes the subject. "Mat, we ought to bring him here. It's time. If we don't, we'll be sorry."

"I'd be sorrier to have imposed something on him he didn't like," Mat says. "I'm not going to do it, Margaret. He'd feel a burden to us. He'd feel dependent and useless, and I don't want to do that to him. He'll be hap-pier staying where he is, paying his own way. If he gets to where he can't do for himself—which I hope he won't—then we'll bring him here."

He speaks more strongly than he feels, for what he has in the back of his mind, what he is not willing to say, is that he is going to put off for as long as possible the extra work that the old man's needs would make for Margaret, whose health is no longer good. Not that what he has said is not true.

"Besides," he says, "he wouldn't come."

And that is true. He would not. He would not allow himself to be meddled with.

"When he needs help, we'll help him," Mat says.

That is what he owes. That is what Old Jack has always given him—

not help that he did not need but always exactly the help he has needed. Mat is sixty-nine years old. Since before he remembers, Jack has been there to be depended on. When Mat was born, Jack was already such a man as few men ever become. He has been faithful all those years. It is a faith that Mat has reciprocated in full. But Jack's faith has been the precedent and model. All his life Mat has had Jack before him, as standard and example, teacher and taskmaster and companion, friend and comforter. When Jack is gone, then Mat will be the oldest of that fellowship of friends and kin of which Old Jack has been for so long the center. He feels the impending exposure of that—nobody standing then between him and the grave. He feels a heavy portent in the imminent breaking of that strand of memory, reaching back into the Civil War, on the end of which Old Jack now keeps so tenuous a hold.

"When he needs it, we'll help him. When he don't, we won't. Ain't that what you'd want?"

"Well," Margaret says. "Hunt him up directly, and see about him, and tell him to come to dinner."

"I'm going to. Now see how far ahead of you I was?"

They laugh. He has quoted his hired hand, Lightning Berlew, who, when given an instruction, always says, "Well, I expect I'm just a little bit ahead of you," and when he has carried it out, usually not very satisfactorily, "Now see how far ahead of you I was?"

Mat gets up and puts on his hat.

"Andy," he says, "take my truck and go help Burley and Jarrat unload what they've got on the wagons." As he leaves, he tips his hat to Margaret.

He goes through the chicken yard gate and across the chicken yard and, by another gate, into the barn lot. The sun is bright now. The river valley is filled with a white billow of fog that trails out into the draws of the upland, growing transparent at its edges.

Lightning is coming up through the pasture from his house, taking his time, and Mat stands to wait for him. Lightning walks, as usual, with his hat brim pulled so low over his eyes that he has to tilt his head far back in order to see; this gives him the vaguely wandering look of a sleepwalker.

After Joe Banion's sudden death of a heart attack in the fall of the year before, Mat was without help for several months. Not long after Joe's burial, his wife, Nettie, had taken his ancient mother and gone off to live with her sister in Cincinnati; that left the house empty, but for weeks Mat was able to find nobody to move in. He could not compete with city jobs for the best of the younger men, and he had not much mind to put up with the worst. But the worst, or near it, was what he finally got: a couple Wheeler Catlett had only heard of, this Lightning and his wife, Sylvania—known, Mat learned later, as Smoothbore—who arrived with all their belongings packed inside of and tied onto an exhausted Chevrolet.

"Tell me niggers been living here," Lightning said engagingly to Mat as he untied the mattress from the car roof.

"If it doesn't suit you," Mat said, "that'll be just fine."

And that was when he learned the first principle of Lightning's character: there is no earthly way to insult him.

"Well," Lightning said, "that ain't nothing a little warshing won't take care of."

The house hadn't really been the issue. If Nettie had been willing to stay, Mat would gladly have built another house to accommodate whatever new help he could get. And he wanted her to stay, not just for Margaret's sake, but because he felt that Nettie—and, even more, Aunt Fanny—belonged there. On the other hand, he could not blame them for leaving. All their kin had gone, and Nettie, who had never learned to drive, felt that she was too old to learn. She wanted to go.

Mat was little enough concerned with "the race problem" in those days, but his bonds with those people went deep. He mourned their departure as he had mourned Joe's death, and missed them painfully when they were gone. In the spring, he and Margaret drove to Cincinnati to see Nettie and the old woman, following Nettie's directions to a red brick tenement near the ball park. It was a Sunday afternoon, hot, the streets lined with people sitting out in chairs and on stoops. They entered a dark, stale-smelling building and climbed to the flat that Nettie had rented on the third floor. Nettie was glad to see them, but quiet, uncertain, strange to them suddenly, no longer held to them by any common ground. She missed Port William; she guessed she always would; she liked very well the new people she worked for. But Mat was most touched by the figure of the old woman who was seated in a sort of alcove between a refrigerator and a window that looked out through the iron of a fire escape at the back of another tenement. She seemed shrunken and resigned, her hands emblematically still, lying in her lap. Where was her garden, where were her plants and speckled hens, where were the long paths of her rambles in the pastures and the woods?

"Aunt Fanny," he said, "you're a mighty long way from home."

"Lord, Mr. Mat," she said, "ain't it the truth!"

They didn't stay long. They had come to offer themselves in some way not well understood and had found themselves to be only strangers, useless to the needs of that place. They threaded the crowd of the street back to where they had left their car. Driving home, Mat was full of a fierce sorrow. If he had spoken, he would have wept. If he could have, if they would have come, he would have brought them home. But he knew that his grief went against history, no stranger to him, whose son was dead in the war; he knew there were not even any words to say. And yet he grieved for Nettie and Aunt Fanny, and for the thousands like them, the exiled children of the land to which their history had been a sacrifice. He knew he had seen the end of what deserved to end better than it had.

And now here comes Lightning Berlew. Mat told him when he moved in that he would expect him to be at the barn at five, before breakfast, to help do the morning chores; he could milk one of the cows for himself.

"I don't want no milk," Lightning said, and he came out no earlier than six-thirty.

Mat offered him a plot of ground and the use of whatever tools he needed to make a garden. Lightning did not even bother to refuse.

Mat said nothing. He had recognized his adversary by then and knew he would have to settle for what he could get, as long as there *was* anything to get. He even knew how it would end: one morning the house would be empty and the old car gone; he would know neither why nor where nor exactly when.

"Morning," he says.

"Hidy!" says Lightning. He is taking his time, the picture of the man of leisure, head tilted back, picking his teeth with the sharpened butt of a burnt match. He comes across the lot and stops in front of Mat.

"Take the tractor and wagon," Mat says, "and go get with Nathan and the others and help them. I'll be there as soon as I can."

Lightning grins his most accommodating grin, his mouth full of silver and gold. With perfect condescension he says, "Well, I expect I'm just a little bit ahead of you." He bites down on the match and reaches into his pocket for his cigarettes.

It makes Mat furious. But, as he often does, he deals with his anger by being correctly generous. He had another thing in mind.

"Lightning," he says, "do you want to kill a hog for yourself this fall?"

"Huh?"

"Do you want a meat hog?"

"I might."

"Well, you can have one of mine. But you'll have to pen it down at your house and feed it out."

"I just might," Lightning says. He goes to get the tractor.

Mat stands still a moment, letting his anger subside, and then starts down toward town.

Lightning will not take the hog. Mat knows that. Then why did he ask? Because it is right? To walk the second mile? Maybe. But maybe, too, for some perverse fascination in seeing the man so steadfastly prove himself a fool. Maybe to allow him to elaborate the accusation there is to be made against him. Mat knows, he knows perfectly well, what Lightning will be doing. At night after work, instead of tending a garden or feeding a hog or doing anything that might be of permanent good to him, instead even of just sitting still, he will have his old Chevrolet pulled into the barn door; he will be lying under it, trying to make it run well enough to get to Hargrave on Saturday night. And while he works on the car, the lady Smoothbore will be sitting there on a bucket, encouraging him, for she apparently has her own reasons for wanting to get to Hargrave. Though the two of them live and work on the place, they have no connection with it, no interest in it, no hope from it. They live, and appear content to live, from hand to mouth in the world of merchandise, connected to it by daily money poorly earned. They worry Mat a good deal more than he will yet admit.

When he comes around the house the hotel porch is vacant and he is startled for a moment. It is as if he had concluded, from Old Jack's immobility earlier, that he would be there whenever he looked again. But if the old man is not on the hotel porch this time of morning, he will be at Jasper Lathrop's store or at Jayber Crow's barbershop. Mat cuts across the road to Jasper's.

The store, whose large front windows face the morning sun, is bright with dust motes whirling in the air from the sweeping that Jasper has just given it. Several women stand at the front counter, talking, waiting to pay for their groceries. But the vital organ of Jasper's store is not the cash register where the women wait; it is the great rusty stove that stands in the back with a bench and several chairs in a half-circle around it. The bench and the chairs have already begun to collect the old men and the idlers who will spend the day loafing among the business places of the town. And standing around the stove, talking and laughing, are several of the younger men, who have stopped by for cigarettes or a visit before going to work, waiting a little, hoping the day will warm and the cold dew dry off the tobacco before they have to get into it. Though there is no fire the chill of the morning is on their minds, and they stand near the stove.

Old Jack is sitting in the angle of the arm and back of the bench, at the end nearest the stove. His coat is misbuttoned so that the left side of the collar rises under his ear. One of the ear flaps of his corduroy cap is dangling. His hands resting on his cane, he is gazing point-blank into the brightness of the front windows. He makes no sign that he has heard, no motion of recognition, when Mat speaks to the other men. Looking at him, Mat feels his absence. He leans over and lays his hand on Old Jack's shoulder.

Way back in Old Jack's mind there is a hillside deep in grass, with trees scattered over it, shading it, and trees around it, and at the foot of the slope a pool of water, still, with the mottled white trunk of a sycamore reflected cleanly in it. He is standing at the edge of the field, looking out into it. He has been there a long time. And now he feels himself touched. A hand has gently grasped his shoulder. It seems to him that it must be Ben Feltner's hand. In the touch of it there is a sort of clarity, a sort of declaration. Not many men Old Jack has known could offer themselves so openly in a touch of the hand. He looks up at Mat, who stands leaning between him and the light. His eyes dazzle.

"Is it Ben?"

"No, Uncle Jack. It's Mat. How are you?"

"I'm all right."

"You feeling all right?"

"Yessir!"

"Well, Margaret said tell you to come to dinner."

"I will that," Old Jack says. He smiles, pleased with the invitation, and with Margaret, whose goodness he trusts but never takes for granted.

And then he reaches out and grips Mat's forearm in an unsteady rough caress. Though Mat's hair is as white as his own, it is very much the gesture of an older man toward a younger one. It is an uncle's gesture, a statement of deeply interested kinship.

"I'm obliged to you, honey."

The wind is stirring the grass of the pasture, and his eyes go back to it. He is at the edge of the field. He would like to walk out into it, he would like to lie down in the shade of one of the trees there by the side of the pool of water. But he is not able to do it now. Though he does not turn his head or look away, he knows that Ruth is standing among the trees behind him. She will not leave him, but neither will she come up beside him and step out with him into the bright field or lie down with him in the shade.

But on his shoulder is the live print, both memory and feeling, of Mat's hand, that is like Ben's, or is Ben's; or the touch of it is Ben's, for what it signifies has shed men's hands like leaves and lived on. It is Ben's kindness, his sweetness of spirit, that has survived in Mat. But there is also in Mat a restless intelligence, an eagerness for things as they ought to be, an anger and grief against things as they are, that he got from his mother. That is Beechum. Mat has never had Ben's patience. Or as much of it as he has ever had, he has had to learn, like Old Jack, out of sorrow.

Jack knew Ben Feltner nearly forty years, and he never saw him in a hurry and he never saw him angry. With Ben that never seemed the result merely of self-control, but rather of an abiding peace that he had made—or maybe a peace that had been born in him—with himself and the world, a willingness to live within the limits of his own fate. Both of them having grown up in his gentle shadow, Jack and Mat have respected and stood in awe of the deep peaceableness they knew in Ben, both of them having failed of it, and at great cost, for so long.

"Jack, my boy," Ben used to say, "the world will still be there when you get to it." To Jack, and later to Mat, when they would be fuming about what might happen, he would say: "Let tomorrow come tomorrow, my boy." Jack was nearly sixty before he learned to do that—but he did learn it, finally. And Ben used to say: "Let the past be gone. Let the dead lie." He would say that, smiling his remote, knowing smile, his hand on his beard. "Let it go by, Jack, my boy." Old Jack never has learned that.

Ben Feltner, that saintly man, dead. Forty-one years in his grave. And Jack Beechum, who was, except in blood and name, his son, has grown old enough to be his father.

"Jack, you want a chew o' tobacker?"

The one hollering in his ear is no stranger to Old Jack, who has known him for five generations, from his grandfathers to his grandsons, but who cannot now call his name, though he can remember his father's name and his grandfather's.

"Nawsir, Irvin," he says. "But thank you, son. I'm obliged to you."

There are only a handful of living names that he can remember. But so direct is his dealing with his failure that he calls the men Irvin, or he calls them son, as he calls all but a few women Suzy or honey. That is his courtesy. They are all young enough to be his sons and daughters now.

Old Jack not having looked at him, the other man returns the cut plug to his pocket and resumes the conversation on his right.

Reminded, Old Jack gets out his own twist of tobacco—the native product, known as "long green"—and cuts off a chew. For a moment he attends to the sounds and smells around him in the store. From the front come the voices of women, laughter. Beside him the talk of the men drones on—something he has passed through and beyond. He does not listen to the words. And his eyes keep their fixed gaze upon the windows straight in front of him. The glare of their morning light, like darkness, suits him as well now as sight. When he wants to, or needs to, he can still see well enough, but it has got so it takes an effort, as though to draw the world together; it seems less and less worth the trouble. His vision, with the finality of some physical change, has turned inward. More and more now the world as it is seems to him an apparition or a cloud that drifts, opening and closing, upon the clear, remembered lights and colors of the world as it was. The world as it is serves mostly to remind him, to turn him back along passages sometimes too well known into that other dead, mourned, unchangeable world that still lives in his mind.

Upon the touch of Mat's hand that bears in it so accurately the touch of Ben's, Old Jack has turned, as on a pivot, back deep into his memory. Now at the age of about eight, three years after the end of the war, he is standing down in the driveway at dusk, looking up at the old house. It is gray for want of paint, and it bears other marks of neglect, as though whatever intelligence inhabits it has turned away and forgotten it. The loss and defeat of the past are still present in it. Already he has learned to stay away from the house as much as he can, shying out of its shadows and memories into the daylight. For him the house is full of the insistent reminding of a past that he never knew, a life that was larger, more coherent and abundant and pleasant than the life he knows. From the drift of subdued talk that has gone on around him he has gathered few facts, nothing at all resembling a sense of history, but rather a vague intimation of an old time of great provisioning, big meals, laughter, bright rooms in which men and women were dancing. And he knows that old time was ended by the war.

Before he ever knew them, his brothers, grown men when he was born, rode off to join the Fourth Kentucky Cavalry. Hamilton and Mathew their names were. He knew that they had gone to fight against the Yankees. Why they went may still be a matter of conjecture. Even in the days of their grandfather the farm had not been a large one; there had never been more than a family or two of slaves; the family had no life-or-death stake in any of the institutions that its two sons undertook to defend. As a boy, Jack merely assumed that they had done as they should have done. Strangers from somewhere else were trying to tell them what to do, and they would not stand for it. Perhaps it was as simple as that. Perhaps it was as inevitable that they should have gone to war as it was that they should have gone to it on horseback, cavalrymen by limitation. It was the choice of the men of their kind; they did not think to do otherwise.

They left, Jack knew, on a morning in September, 1862, after the tobacco had been housed, having refused to sign with the recruiters until the crop was in. Though Jack was too young—he was later repeatedly told that he was too young—to remember them, he has nevertheless kept all his life a strange, unfocused vision of their departure. Was he only told about it, or did he actually see it, held up in his mother's or in Nancy's arms to watch them go? It is a clear bright cool morning, the taste of fall in the air. The two of them, Ham and Mat, ride down the driveway under the shadows of the trees, their horses, a chestnut and a bay, going side by side. Each of them has a roll of blankets tied behind his saddle; each carries a rifle across his saddlebow. Their hats are tilted forward to shade their eyes, for they are riding into the sun. What did they look like? He does not know. They move as in a sort of peripheral vision; when he attempts to concentrate his memory upon them, to examine them as with a direct look, they fade away. It seems to him that as they ride to the end of the driveway and turn onto the road and go out of sight they do not look back. It seems to him that as he watches them they have already seen the house for the last time and their backs are turned to it forever. This is not simply the knowledge of retrospect; because the vision of their departure met the knowledge of their deaths in the anachronistic mind of a child, the two have fused, so that it seems to him, in his vision, that he watches them depart with the clear foreknowledge that they will not return. And they did not. Mat was killed the next month in their regiment's first engagement, at the Battle of Perryville, and Ham in Morgan's third fight at Cynthiana in June of 1864.

He does not remember any of the circumstances surrounding the news of Mat's death. Long before Mat's life became a fact to him, his death was also a fact. But he can remember when they heard of the death of Ham. Jack was four then. Mainly he remembers that for two or three days after the news came he was not permitted to see his mother. His father sat long at a time by the dead hearth in the front room, looking at the floor. Nancy and the cook kept Jack in the kitchen with them, taking him on walks outside when he got restless. In the house they spoke in whispers. That whispering has always stayed in his mind, an awesome portent, full of the intimation of tragedies and mysteries. Why would a man be killed? What happened to him then? How long was forever? And he remembers Nancy hugging him and rocking him at night beside one of the upstairs windows. He knew that she was crying.

And before the spring of the next year his mother was dead, and they had buried her among the tilting stones and the old cedars in the grave-yard at Port William. It has always been of heavy significance to him that she died before the war's end, in the bitterness and sorrow, and what seems to him to have been the darkness, of its last winter.

And so by the war's end the old house was infected with a sense of loss and diminishment, and with a quietness. It was as though, entering one of the still rooms at dusk, the boy could hear the solemn echoes of a failed delight, or the departing footsteps of his brothers, whose coats still hung on pegs in one of the upstairs closets. But more than anything else the quietness of the house bore the recollection of the quietness that had surrounded the final long illness of his mother.

As he thinks of himself standing there in the driveway more than eighty years ago, he feels again a dread that was inescapable then and that he never forgot. The memory is without antecedent; perhaps the recollection has already lasted longer than the event. It is getting dark. The swifts have begun dropping into the chimneys. It is the time when the sorrows of the house return to it and brood in it. Of all who were once there, only he and Nancy and his father are left. There will come a time when Jack's own vigor and spirit will overpower the melancholy of the house—a time when, with a bravado almost intimidating to himself, he will appropriate his brothers' forsaken clothes and wear them out. But that time is yet long away. Now the house will be full of the presence of an unappeasable sorrow, and he dreads to enter it, and he knows he must. Soon now they will be calling him.

By his sixth year Jack's mind had already learned what would be one of its characteristic motions, turning away from the house, from the losses and failures and confinements of his history, to the land, the woods and fields of the old farm, in which he already sensed an endlessly abounding and unfolding promise. He stayed outdoors as much as he could, following the men to the fields when they would let him, wandering the woods and the creeks when they would not. Outside, away from the diminished and darkened house, there had already begun the long arrival of what was to be. Away from the house he was free; he felt the power of his own moods and inclinations; he followed the promptings of his curiosity about whatever was going on in the fields and the woods. He was always in somebody's way, trying to see what was happening. "*Get back!*" they would have to be telling him. "Get out the way! How can I see what I'm doing with yo' big head stuck in the way?" The black hired men corrected and instructed him, usually with good humor; they were resigned to this, knowing that if they did not do it nobody else was apt to. They taught him to work. As the price of staying with them he learned what they wanted him to know. What he wanted from them, what he asked of the fields where they went to work, was relief from the failed history that had been shut away from time, stalled and turned back upon itself, in the house. He wanted that sense of the continuous arrival of time and weather that one might get from standing day and night on the top of a hill.

There would come times, later, when he would have to turn from the hazards and bewilderments of that implacable arrival, always hastening as he grew older, back toward his history. Needing experience older than his own in order to know what to expect and what was possible, he would turn to Ben Feltner, as later the younger men would turn to him.

His father had suffered too much from his experience, had felt too great a futility in it, to be able to offer it to the boy. Instead he made a sort of pet of him. From the time Jack was three years old until he got big enough to want to be busy on his own, his father kept him with him whenever he was able; he would take him to work with him, or lift him up onto the saddle in front of him when he went on horseback. Sitting at the table after a meal or in the front room before bedtime, he would pull the boy up into his lap to pat him and hug him. But for all that, it was a strangely silent relationship that the two of them had. Jack said little for fear that he would touch or rouse the pain that he sensed in his father. And his father, because he was weary of his life, or because he had grown fearful of such knowledge as he had, said only what was necessary: "Come on" or "Jump down" or "Yes" or "No." Sometimes they would ride to town and back, the boy straddling the saddlebow in front of his father—Jack can still remember, can still feel, his father's hand and forearm crooked around his waist—and they would never say a word. Or they would be together half a day in the field, just as silently, while the father worked and the boy played near him. At those times he was always aware that his father kept a kind of vigil over him. He would look up from his play to see his father standing and gazing at him; his father would smile and nod, or he would raise his hand in a kind of salute, as though he were watching from a great distance.

But he was never comfortable with his father, who had always about him the melancholy of the house and its deaths. He got from his strange companionship with his father the sense of a forbearing, almost tender kindness that later he would remember with pleasure and with regret. But what he consciously learned and understood of manhood he got from Ben Feltner.

It was when Jack was eight that Ben began his courtship of Nancy—a courtship that would last, by the dispensation of Ben's patience, for eleven years, while Nancy fulfilled and completed her duties as the woman of her father's house. They were married in 1879, after Nancy had buried her father, and mothered and brought up and kept house for her young brother until she thought he could be left to look after himself. So far as Jack knew there was never a formal proposal. When the time came—the three of them were sitting in the kitchen, having eaten—Ben said: "Jack, my boy, I believe it's time we put you on your own." And Nancy, blushing, looking out the window, said, "Yes, Jack, I think it's time."

She was as much a mother to him as he ever needed her to be. She taught him his manners, saw to it that he got what schooling was available to him, and when there was no school she set him problems in arithmetic and had him read to her from the Bible. When he balked at that or at any other task, she turned not to their father but to Ben. "Why, Jack," Ben would say, "it's no more than ought to be asked of a man." Ben took care not to have Jack in sight too much of the time. But when Jack was in Ben's sight, he obeyed him; it never occurred to him not to, for Ben was just and he knew how much to ask.

From the war until the father's death the farm deteriorated. At first Jack was too young to give any care to it, and his father had become satisfied to do only what was necessary to hold it together and to stay alive on it. By the time Jack finally got big enough to be of use, the old man had abandoned even that effort; his only urgency by then was to keep anything more from happening. But the place was going badly downhill, and they were borrowing money. As he approached manhood, seeing what needed to be done, Jack began to chafe and fret against the restraints of his father's obsession. "Goddamn it," he would say to Ben, "all he says is no." And out of the shadows of so many years he can hear Ben: "Be easy, now. Be a little easy."

It is growing dark, and the boy, Jack Beechum, is standing as he has been standing for a long time, the stones of the driveway beginning to press painfully against the soles of his bare feet. He is looking up the driveway at the gray walls of the house that would not be painted again until the time of his own marriage. (His marriage, the beginning of his story, when Ruth would come to the house as his bride—he would have it painted and put right by then.) The trees of the yard have grown shadowy, the leaves now indistinct in their mass. The work is done at the barn, the men have gone home for the night, the place has fallen quiet. He feels the melancholy of the old house reach out toward him and touch him like a draft of cold air.

And then, behind him, he hears a horse stepping along the road. He turns and sees a man turn in at the gate on a high-headed bay. The man, whom he has seen before but does not know, rides up beside the boy and stops. He is a young man with good eyes and a heavy brown beard, whose squareness of build and breadth of shoulder make him appear less tall than he is. He leans forward, his two hands crossed over the pommel of the saddle—at ease, as though he might mean to stay quite a while right there.

"My boy," he says, "might your sister be home?"

"She ain't ever anyplace else," Jack says.

Ben clears his throat. "I see." He raises his head and looks for some time at what is now only the silhouette of the house, as though he is making some intricate calculation about it. Does he want to go to the house? Or not?

"I see," he says. And then, as if remembering something clean forgot, he looks down again to where the boy is standing, by the left foreleg of the horse, and smiles. "Can you show me where to put my horse?"

"Yes sir."

"Do you want to ride?"

"Yes sir.

The man reaches down with his right hand. "Well, take a hold of that, and give a jump."

Jack does as he is told, and is swung up and behind the man's back. It is done powerfully, all in one motion, and the man has made a friend.

"I'm Ben Feltner," he says. "Who are you?"

"Jack Beechum."

"That's what I thought."

Jack settles himself behind the saddle and takes hold of the waist of Ben's coat. There is something comfortable about this man, whose hat and big shoulders now loom up so, a new horizon, in the fading light, who smells of horse sweat and pipe smoke.

"Are you set?" Ben asks.

"Yes sir."

Ben clucks to the horse.

"You came to see my sister?" Jack asks, wondering a little, for few people come to the house to see any of them any more.

"Your sister Nancy Beechum?"

"Yes sir."

"Well, I came to see her."

And they ride up the driveway toward the house, forbidding to Jack because of other people's sorrows, but where he will come to sorrows enough of his own. As he pictures it now, even back in that far-off old time it seems already expectant of her who was to come.

Three : Ruth

He knows too well the way his mind is taking him—his mind that, like a hunting dog backtracking through the country, keeps turning back and turning back, tracing out the way it has come. As if it will be any help to it to know. His mind, he thinks, would do well to settle down and be quiet, for pretty soon he is going up on the hill for the long sleep that most people he knows have already gone off to, and there is not a lot that a man's mind can do about that. He has no fear of death. It is coming, there is nothing to be done about it, and so he does not think about it much. It is the unknown, and he has come to the unknown before. Sometimes it has been very satisfying, the unknown. Sometimes not. Anyhow, what would a man his age propose to do instead of die? He has been around long enough to know that death is the only perfect cure for what ails mortals. After you have stood enough you die, and that is all right.

And so he does not think of death more often than necessary, and he can quit thinking about it any time he wants to. He does not think of what lies ahead. He will leave that to the Old Marster. And there are days, less frequent now that he has so little will to attend to what is going on, when he lives caught up and enclosed in the present. He is like an old dog then—"Son," he said to Burley Coulter, who told Mat, "I'm just like an old dog. Got nothing on my mind but gravy, and now and then a fly"—sleeping a light sleep that allows him to remain aware of the warmth and comfort of whatever place he has come to, or waking and looking with idle and remote interest at the scene that his fading eyes have blurred and withdrawn from. Those are his best days, he knows, though they leave behind them a taint of idleness that troubles him and that has kept two such days from ever occurring together.

But the present is small and the future perhaps still smaller. And what his mind is apt to do is leap out of that confinement, like an old dog, still strong, that has been penned up and then let loose in the one countryside that it knows and that it knew for a long time. But it is like an old dog possessed by an old man's intelligent ghost that remembers all it has seen and done and all the places it has known, and that goes back to haunt and lurk in those places. Some days he can keep it very well in hand, just wandering and rummaging around in what he remembers. He is amazed at what he comes upon that he thought he had forgot. He can remember dates and names and prices and measures and dimensions of all kinds. He can remember the way men looked and the way they moved and how they worked and what they did. He can remember the faces and the bodies of women, and the playing of certain fiddlers; at times he can play a whole tune out in his head just like a Victrola. He can remember crops, their quality and weight and what they brought. He can remember the markings and the color and the conformation and the disposition and the gait of any number of horses and mules. He can remember, in detail down to the markings of their faces, bunches of cattle that he owned, and can move among them in his mind, looking them over. Sometimes he can recover a whole day, with the work he did in it, and the places and the animals and the people and even the words that belong to it.

And that is all right. But there have been some bad days in his life, too. Plenty of them, and it is hard to keep his mind, ranging around the way it does, from crossing the track of his hard times. Though he would a lot rather let them lie still and be gone, once his mind strikes into his old troubles there is no stopping it; he is in his story then, watching, as he has helplessly done many times before, to see how one spell of trouble and sorrow led to another. Once he has started he has to go on, yet one more time, to the end. He knows now that, do what he may, his history is about to wash over his mind again, like water over a field under a hard rain. He will think again of Ruth and of Clara and of Rose; he will have to consider once more the way things might have been, and the way they were. Too old to work and get around, he can do nothing but let it come.

But he will put it off a little too, if he can. He unbuttons his coat now, and probes with his finger into the bib pocket of his overalls, and draws out his watch by its plaited thong. It is 9:25. He looks around. The other loafers are gone from the benches and chairs, having drifted out to the street or into another of the stores. He is the only one there—he and Jasper Lathrop who is sitting on the counter by the cash register, his legs dangling, reading the paper. The sun has long ago quit shining straight into the front windows. Now its light lies richly on the floor under Jasper's feet. The town has assumed the raptness that comes upon it after the morning work of the households and the fields has begun.

He looks at the watch again and replaces it, and draws out a small notebook and a pencil. Both the notebook and the pencil bear the legend "Reed & Spaulding, Livestock Brokers, Bourbon Stockyards, Louisville, Ky." That's where he sells his stock. Whenever he and Elton Penn go down to sell their lambs or their hogs or their cattle, and have seen them sold and have come in out of the yards to the brokers' office to wait for their check, one of the girls at the counter—a pretty little thing—always says, "Mr. Beechum, would you like a new notebook and pencil?" And Old Jack gets up, taking his hat off, and goes up to her window. "I would that, honey. I thank you kindly." And she gives them to him and pats his hand. She says, "How have you been, Mr. Beechum?" And he says, "Mighty well, thank you," for, the obvious qualifications aside, that is the truth. "Well, you certainly are *looking* fine," she says. And convinced that she is not telling the truth, but that he is, he says, "Well, sweet thing, you're as fine a looking a little woman as ever I laid eyes on." She likes it when he says that.

Nearly half the notebook is filled with figures engraved deeply into the pages with the blunt point of the pencil. This is where Old Jack figures up how things are going on his farm. Some of the figures are real, some are estimated, but there are only figures. No words. Each page bears the tracks of an entirely new story of how things may turn out. They always turn out well; he never quits his figuring, raising the incomes and reducing the outgoes, until the final sum pleases him. This work of his frequently leads to an uproarious argument with Wheeler Catlett, Mat's son-in-law, Old Jack's kinsman by marriage and his lawyer and his friend. Wheeler does not estimate, at least not about what has been earned, and so the form of their business dealings has come to be this terrible argument, which they both enjoy a great deal. "God Almighty, no!" Wheeler will say. "Where in hell did you ever get such a figure as that?" And Old Jack will say, "Out of my head, by God, that knew this business before you were born, and had a hat on it three hours before you were out of bed."

His trouble—which he knows that Wheeler knows—is that he cannot remember any figures that came into his head less than twenty years ago. He can remember how many steers he had in 1925 and what he paid for them and what they weighed when he sold them and how much they brought, but he cannot remember how many he has now. So he guesses. Guessing, he begins to figure up what his cattle have cost him, and what they are likely to bring.

The front door opens and he looks up. It is Burley Coulter who has come in. Seeing him there, Burley stops and gives him the river boatman's salute, solemnly waving both arms in and out over his head, as though they are divided by too great a span of water to be able to speak. Old Jack snorts in amusement. That is Burley's way, to be carrying on some kind of foolishness. But a good man, too, with a good head on his shoulders, who has done a lot of work in his time.

Burley continues his greeting long enough both to enjoy it and to have it appreciated, and then comes back to the bench.

"How are you, old scout?"

"I'm all right. How're you, Burley?"

"Best you ever saw."

"Ay God, I know it! You're a good one."

And his old daddy before him was a good one, old Dave. But Jarrat, Burley's brother, is the one who is like Dave. Burley takes more after his mother's people, the Humstons. He laughs like old man Whit Humston, his grandaddy on his mother's side.

"There's a lot of Humston in you, Burley."

"Well, I can't help it."

"They were good people. Had a lot of wit about 'em. I knew 'em all."

"Well, I expect I'd better go," Burley says. But he adds, knowing the old man will be interested, "Me and Jarrat stayed home this morning and housed up a couple of loads we had to leave on the wagons last night. Andy helped us. We're all going to pitch in on Nathan and Mat's this morning."

"Is Elton there?"

"He's supposed to be."

Burley turns and starts out, and then snaps his fingers and turns back to the counter. "What I came for was smokes."

Grinning at him, Jasper tosses a pack of cigarettes onto the counter. Burley puts down his money and puts the cigarettes in his shirt pocket. He shakes his head.

"A man with a forgetter like I got—his mind ain't burdened."

He goes out.

It is time Old Jack was moving too. He will be nearly too stiff to get up if he does not move now. He gets up and starts to the door. As unobtrusively as possible, Jasper opens it for him.

"Thank you, boy. Thank you, Irvin," Old Jack says, raising his hand to Jasper as he goes by.

As he steps into the open he is aware, as always, of the sudden widening of his horizon, the lighted sky above his head; he gives his shoulders a slight lift and shrug, as though having just rid himself of a confining garment. He can see Burley and Jarrat Coulter driving through the gate up at Mat's with a tractor and two empty wagons. Old Jack hates tractors. They seem to him suddenly to be everywhere, roaring and stinking. With a sort of fierce grace, he has kept his hatred to himself, not wanting to interfere with a world that he is so nearly out of. But he hates their heaviness, their hulking and graceless weight. They remind him of groundhogs. They have the look about them of being just ready to burrow into the ground.

For a moment he glimpses a load of tobacco drawn by the team of black mare mules.

Stepping. *Ay! Lord!*

His thoughts have left him for another place and time. For the day it is and the time of year and the sound of the wagons going out have alerted him, as if at the sound of an old song in the distance, to the time when his strength was light in him.

Oh, he was something to look at then! He admits it now with a candor too impersonal to need modesty. There were days in his early manhood when it seems to him he walked in the air. He stood and moved with a lightness that was almost flight. His hand moved effortless as his eye. He looks back upon himself as he was, exulting in his great strength, indulgent of his eagerness and desire, as he might, had he been so favored, have looked upon a grandson. But he has had neither son nor grandson. It is the blessing and the trial of his old age that his mind goes back to inhabit again and again the body of the man he was.

In 1888 he was twenty-eight years old. Three years before, both his parents dead, the older children dead or gone from home, he had bought from his sister Nancy, now Nancy Feltner, her interest in the land his father and grandfather had farmed, and on which he had been born. Several years yet away from his marriage, he lived alone in the old house; an elderly Negro woman, Aunt Ren, the wife of the hired hand who had been his father's slave, came in daily to cook and to keep the mostly forsaken rooms. The place was run down, the bank's interest having fed heavily on it during the father's last years, and the debt against it was large. But in those days Jack was free of other obligations, he was strong, he had the sort of overreaching intelligence that pleases itself with difficulty, and so hardship and debt did not burden him. What moved him then was a sense of the possibilities that lay yet untouched in his land. The rest of his own life seemed to him to lie unborn in the soil of the old farm.

By Jack's time, the farm had been reduced by his father's money troubles to about a hundred and fifty acres. It was bounded in front by the road, and on the other three sides by the winding courses of Birds Branch and two of its tributaries. The hollows of these streams were narrow, offering little bottom land for crops. But there were cleared pastures on the slopes above them. Above the openings of pasture, where the hill steepened, the land was in woods. Wooded draws cut deeply into the upland, so that the long ridge that formed the backbone of the farm was broken into three almost symmetrical broad hilltops. The upland fields had been divided from the steeper land by stone fences that followed faithfully the contour of the ground, keeping the line where the steeps gentled at the top of their rise. The house with its company of barns and outbuildings faced the road, set back from it in a yard shaded by big sugar maples and oaks. It was a farm that required a great deal of care, so much of it being steep. But its design had been cunningly laid out to preserve the land and to be convenient and pleasing to the eye.

He had known no other place. From babyhood he had moved in the openings and foldings of the old farm as familiarly as he moved inside his clothes. But after the full responsibility of it fell to him, he saw it with a new clarity. He had simply relied on it before. Now when he walked in his fields and pastures and woodlands he was tramping into his mind the shape of his land, his thought becoming indistinguishable from it, so that when he came to die his intelligence would subside into it like its own spirit.

The work satisfied something deeper in him than his own desire. It was as if he went to his fields in the spring, not just because *he* wanted to, but because his father and grandfather before him had gone because *they* wanted to—because, since the first seeds were planted by hand in the ground, his kinsmen had gone each spring to the fields. When he stepped into the first opening furrow of a new season he was not merely fulfilling an economic necessity; he was answering the summons of an immemorial kinship; he was shaping a passage by which an ancient vision might pass once again into the ground.

He remembers those days for their order, the comeliness of the shape his work made in each one of them as it passed. It was an order that came of the union in him of skill and passion, the energy that would not be greater in him than it was then. But it also came of solitude. He had no help except for the aged Negro man, Uncle Henry, whose greatest usefulness by then was to tend the garden and do the chore work around the barn. That set Jack's mind free in the fields, and except at the times of planting and harvest, when he teamed with his neighbors, he worked alone. His solitude assured that his work would have the coherence of his character. He went free of the awkwardness that comes of the mismatching of two men working together. He knew how much work he could do in a day, and how to do it. It was as if he worked always in the open then, and there was a clarity between him and the eye of heaven. He was in the clear with those gods of the fields about whom the men of his kind spoke sparingly and carefully: the Old Marster, whose inscrutable ways were known to Job; and the sun, Old Hanner, indifferently harsh and kind.

It was only on Saturday evening that the strenuous order of his workdays opened to let him escape—or be driven out by the desire that the very sunset of that day made strong in him, for women, for company, for music, for the free exuberance that his workdays did not allow. Most Saturday nights he knew of a dance to be held at a house or schoolhouse, sometimes miles away. And he would go, washing and dressing after work in haste to be gone, often not waiting to eat. For he loved the music and the mingling, the drink and talk and laughter of the dances they used to have back in those old days. Women moved him. And he was a man subject to music as grass to wind. He was a gifted dancer. He could be carried away.

He comes alone and late to where the horses stand hitched at the yard fence of a house brightly lighted, the air around it filled with the high-riding tune of "Wildwood Flower." And he goes in to where the light is and the bystanders ringing the room and the fiddle urging from its corner; a girl's hands are held out to him and he takes them, the music lifting him, and steps light into the circle of the dancers. Carried away in the wild drift of the dance that will bear him through the night, he forgets where he is. He has to reach down with his feet to tread the floor.

In the casual way of men to whom such things come by nature, he had got to be handy with the women—handy enough to have caused himself more trouble than he did, had he talked about it. In a crowd of strangers at some dance or gathering far from home there would pass between him and some one of the women a strand of delight that would draw them together to the dark that he loved to let himself go thoughtless into.

It was his own extravagant nature that he traveled in, and he was learning its formidable distances and perilous heights. He did not mind the going. That was light and eager. It was the coming back that required a change and a recognition that troubled and vaguely frightened him. He felt the strangeness of his absence. He returned with the anxiety of one who has been absent a year, considering what might have gone wrong. The few mornings when he returned to find that something in fact *had* gone wrong, he knew the anger of regret for which he could find no fitting act. Though he did not know it then, it was an emotion that would be one of the powerful themes of his life.

It was not only in Jack's character but also in his place and time that
the way was so ill prepared and the going so difficult between the wake-
ful days that he aspired to and the joys and transports of the night. How
much his tragedy that has been he well knows, now that his lightness
and most of his light too have gone from him, and he has learned by
their loss to look back and know and lament the single vital strand that
bound the day and the night together. From where he stands now, sixty
years and more and a long descent from the best of his nights and days,
he knows that those nights of mirth and music issued out of and cele-
brated his strenuous days, and that his days sought an indispensable por-
tion of their meaning in those nights. But back so long ago, a young man
who had in him such a devotion to the light and such a calling to the
dark, he had yet to learn much that he knows now.

He looks up at Mat's to see if he can see any sign of Elton Penn. This
is the seventh year now that Elton has lived on Old Jack's place—a proven
man, young as he still is. He keeps tight up against his work all the time,
and does it right. And not because somebody expects it. He does it
because he expects it of himself. He has the right kind of head on his
shoulders. He has become the last keen delight of Old Jack's life—the
inheritor of his ways. He has been willing to listen, and Old Jack has
taught him some things. He has made a kind of son of him.

He does not see anybody. They are all in the field. And he lets the
world return into its blurred distance, aware as often before of the tragedy that all his true heirs—all who have had a use for such a head as his—
have come to him as if by chance, without the heat of his own desire.

There was something he had in mind to do. And then it hits him
again, the pain of his filled bladder ringing in him like a bell. He heads up
the street, careful of the divided and tilted sections of the old pavement.
At the back of an outbuilding behind the hotel he relieves himself, and
then he comes back along the shady corridor between buildings into the
open sunshine of the street. The day has turned warm now, will be hot
by noon. He goes under the shade trees in front of the hotel and back
into the sun, past Jasper's and the drugstore. At the corner of the barbershop he has to stop and rest. He turns to face the street and props himself
with the cane.

He is going on horseback down the driveway. It is a Sunday morning early in the May of 1889. The weather is clear and warm. There has been rain, and the littlest streams are brimming and shining. The spring is at its height. The grass of the yard and the pastures is lush, the green of it so new that it gleams in the sun. The trees are heavily leafed, their new growth still tender, unblemished. The whole country lies beneath an intricate tapestry of bird song. He is on his way to church—one of the pilgrimages that he occasionally makes in uneasy compensation for the extravagances of Saturday night.

But he hardly feels like a penitent. He feels good, as much wrought upon by the joyousness of that morning as a bird or a tree. He is wearing a black suit, fairly new, so made that he keeps a continuous awareness in his waist and shoulders of the perfection of its fit. And he is riding as fine a saddle horse as he ever owned—a big red sorrel gelding, groomed until the light melts and flows over his neck and shoulders as he moves. Jack feels himself contained and carried in the brilliant harmony that can occur between a gifted horseman and an excellent horse. He looks his best, and none of the considerable force of his good looks is lost on him. It was not until he got old that Jack was willing to admit, even in his own mind, the extent of the pride that he took then in his looks. But there it is. He is in the service of nature, a cock bird plumed and preened, the world his reflection. The service he is going to, he has already arrived at. The morning sermon will be *his* occasion, no matter what he supposed when he decided to go. His hands delicately enact the connection between his own strength and that of the horse. Under him the horse moves powerfully and lightly, his every move suggestive of an abounding energy suppressed by the rider's hand. And Jack feels that same checked and conserved abundance in himself, his shoulders pressing against the good broadcloth of his suit. The whole country around him, in fact, is full of it, the abounding of energy and desire, threatening to overwhelm the forms of growth and song that provide for its release; to accommodate it, the birds must repeat their songs over and over so that the air around his head seems swollen with music.

The road follows a long backbone of the upland, rising and falling with the rises and falls of the ground. At the tops of the rises he can see the steeple of the church in town lifting white out of the green cloud of massed treetops, and smaller, beyond the steeple, the cupola of Ben Feltner's barn. Beyond town he can see the misty opening of the river valley. And then he comes to the Birds Branch Church, a neat white building without a steeple, standing on a stone-walled terrace leveled in the hillside. The old oaks throw over its roof and walls the new shadows of the spring. He rides into the churchyard and hitches his horse among the others already there. The service has begun; the congregation is singing "Amazing Grace, how sweet the sound," the song pouring out the open doors and windows of the old church, mingling, beyond its intent, into the wild fecundity of the day.

He steps in and finds a place on the end of a back bench. Fresh from the outdoors, he breathes in and examines the rich mixture of smells: the staleness of the old building more often closed than open, the smell of the ground and of new growth from outside, the odors of soap and clean clothes, and, insistent among the rest, the perfumes and sachets of the women. The service continues to prayers and more singing; the collection is taken; the sermon begins. Jack settles himself as comfortably as he can in the angle of the arm and the back of the bench. He is both there and not there, full of pleasure in the day and a sort of idle interest in what is going on around him. He is not listening to the sermon. The sermon is merely a presence, a distant drone among the humming and singing that the air is already full of, borne away on the fragrance that draws through the windows.

His sight drifts and gazes upon the heads ranged in front of him, picking out, recognizing, the heads of the girls and young women. His consciousness hovers and moves now over the congregation, like a bee over a patch of flowers, in search of nectar, alert to what is bright and sweet and open.

And now, five or six rows in front of him, he sees a head he doesn't recognize—as beautiful a head, surely, as he will ever see, the hair heavy and rich, the color of honey and butter, but worn with a simplicity, a lack of ostentation, that moves him strangely. There is something about that head that is both opulent and innocent. For a moment, though he does not move, he strains toward her, looking at her as though to memorize every tiny detail of the look of her; it is a memory that will stay with him, clear as his eye was then, for sixty-three years. And then he settles back into himself. Well! But he tells himself to wait a while; no use being

misled by a head of hair, fine as that one is. There is a cautionary
instinct—the deliberately critical eye of the experienced stockman, perhaps—warning him to make no quick judgments, to be careful, to take
his time. But he sits through the rest of the meeting with all his senses
sharpened and expectant, like a hungry man who has had a whiff of a
good meal. She is sitting with the family of Perry Clemmons from down
in the river bottom not far from Port William—come visiting kinfolks,
he supposes.

The sermon ends. They rise to sing the final hymn. As the girl stands
and turns a little to share her book with one of the daughters of the family, Jack can see—he has been waiting to see—that she is well made, her
figure ample but delicately and neatly formed. Again the sight of her
moves him, touches him as though inside his skin, and he feels a clench-
ing and sinking of his vitals. His imagination is moving over her now like
a water witch over a buried vein of water, sensing beneath the yellow
summer dress she wears the presence of her body, both marvelously rich
and marvelously fine. And still he tells himself to wait. Wait, for there is
more yet to be seen.

The singing ends. The preacher says the benediction. The order of
the congregation loosens within itself. A stir rises as neighbors turn to
speak to each other, and then there begins a general movement toward
the door. Jack moves out of the way, but only to step back and stand
again between the back of the bench and the wall, just inside the door.
He watches the girl move out from between the benches and then step
into the aisle. When she turns to face the door, because Jack is then
directly in her line of vision, they look straight into each other's eyes.
The veins of his head dilate with the suddenness of a blow, so deeply has
he prepared himself and desired to see her face and so openly do their
eyes meet. The look holds only an instant, for she smiles a little confus-
edly at the force of his stare and looks away. But he does not look away.
Her face is astonishingly fine, fair, lightly freckled across the nose, the
eyes gray, grave, and clear. It is a face almost austerely beautiful. But what
seems to him most remarkable is its innocence. It is a face that does not
seem to belong at all to such a woman's body as hers. There is in her
countenance no acknowledgment, as there is perhaps no awareness, of
the great earthly power of her beauty that has so shaken him that he can-

not look away. The look of her reminds him of a young girl on a horse, simply trusting herself to a power she has not measured and does not know.

She neither looks at him again nor avoids looking at him. She comes on up the aisle and past him and out the door. He sees now that his long, oblivious gaze at the girl has been noticed by certain ones of the congregation. "Well," he thinks. "Well, then, if she doesn't know, she'll be told." He moves into the aisle and goes out. He does not look again at the girl, but goes to his horse.

He is twenty-nine years old, accustomed to an exacting manhood. He ceased to be childish before he ceased to be a child; he knew too much solitude and came to a workman's competence too early. By the time he had reached the age when a young man might be thought puerile or callow, he had already lived past that possibility. And so what he does now, though it is full of pride, has none of the brashness of showing off. The face and the body of this strange girl have so entered his mind that from head to foot he feels luminous and light with the thought of her. He wants the attention and respect of such a woman, but he pretends to nothing, the possibility of pretense does not cross his mind. His pride is simply that of an accomplished man who wants to be seen and known for what he is. He loosens the rein and backs the gelding clear of the other horses. Feeling the bit, the horse is suddenly alert as a deer, quivering to be gone, but held back as if by the mere presence of his rider. And then, as Jack gathers the reins over the gleaming withers and steps into the stirrup, the horse moves off in long, powerful, somehow delicate strides, seeming to rise to meet his rider as he settles onto his back, one with him. There is a breathless perfection about it, as though two powerful opposites have met without impact or sound. There is swiftness but not haste, strength but not violence. It is all power and light, that beginning, like the beginning of the flight of a falcon. Yes, there were watchers—Jack knew it, though he never turned his head.

He never turned his head. And all week, though he thought of her, each time with the quickening and sinking that he had felt in the church, he did nothing different for the girl's sake. The week's work held him, and he gave himself to it. But on Saturday evening he did something different. Instead of going off to a dance that he knew about, and instead of staying at home as he sometimes did when he felt the dances to be taking him too far, he went out to town and bought a few groceries and loafed and talked. He had given his whole attention to the girl again and he was watching for her. But though he waited until long past bedtime she did not come, and he rode home, late, strangely disappointed and anxious. He had, by bringing the talk around to the subject of a good brood mare that belonged to Perry Clemmons, discovered the girl's name: Ruth Lightwood.

The name changed him. He was now a man who knew the name of what he wanted; he had spoken it to himself. The next day he went to the church again—afraid that she would have finished her visit and returned he did not know where. But there she was. Again, when the sermon was over, he placed himself in her way. This time, he noticed, she did openly look at him, and behind the mask he had made of his face he exulted. He saw that she had asked about him, for she looked at him not just with interest but with something of the curiosity of a child, her eyes asking what manner of man might do what she had heard he had done. He did not wait, that time, for her to walk past him, but turned and went out ahead of her and, without looking back, mounted his horse as before and rode away. But by then his mind had turned from aspiration to labor; as he rode home he was thinking of the possible worth of a mare like that one of Perry Clemmons's that, bred to the right kind of jack, would have a good mule.

And a little before ten o'clock on Monday morning he was on the road again, shaved, wearing his best everyday clothes. He went to Port William and down the hill and upriver through the bottoms to Perry Clemmons's. He found Mr. Clemmons, with several of his men, planting corn in a long bottom near the river. They talked at the row end, and Jack mentioned his interest in the mare. He let himself be traded out of the good mule that he had decided beforehand to offer as a last resort, and then was invited to dinner as he had expected.

When he came into the dining room with his host, Ruth was already seated at the table with Mrs. Clemmons and her daughters. He saw that she was surprised to see him, and he saw that she blushed, pleased and embarrassed about it. He grinned at her, admitting everything: that he was there, that he had made himself something of a rascal, that he would do it again for her sake. But not to embarrass her further, he paid no special attention to her during the meal. He took part in the talk, minded his manners, praised the meal, ate moderately, and forbore to linger, though he wanted to, after Mr. Clemmons got up to return to the field. The women had already begun to clear the table, and as Jack followed Mr. Clemmons out of the room he hung back a little, giving himself a chance to meet Ruth in the hall. She came out of the dining room with her hands full of glasses. He bowed slightly and smiled.

"Oh!" she said.

"Fine to have you in this part of the country, Miss Ruth."

"Thank you."

"How long you going to stay?"

He intended that to be a little too much, and it was.

"I've heard about you, *Mister* Beechum."

But then, as if she wanted her chastisement to be acceptable and instructive to him, as if she could not bear *only* to punish him, she offered him a hesitant smile as she turned away.

He knew what she had heard. Or he could guess. That he was a dancer, a drinker, a wencher, a fighter. He had been none of these ruinously and it had not occurred to him to feel guilty. But he knew that she held him guilty, and he knew that her censure would not quibble over degrees. For the first time, then, he felt the force of a past that was his own, and he felt it with a peculiar mixture of regret and defiance that would become familiar to him. But he thought, too, of her smile, and of her eyes with their childish candor, as though she only observed the effect of a desire that she did not know she had caused. He wanted to see her eyes own and acknowledge and accept, yes, and celebrate the heat that she had stirred in him, her power over him. As he rode home, leading the old mare, the prospective mother of mules, he was saying to himself, "Well well well. Well. Well well."

He had to go back to deliver the mule, but in his parting conversation with Mr. Clemmons he had deliberately put that off until the middle of the week, so as to draw out and conserve the pleasure of looking forward to it. He guessed that his chances were fairly poor, but when he went back, toward sundown on Wednesday, she was watching for him though she pretended not to be, and this time they spoke at some length on the porch as he was leaving, Jack pressing her to agree to let him come again, she putting him off with veiled allusions to his misdeeds—which she would not accuse him of, he knew later, because she could not bring herself to name them.

And yet they fascinated her. Their darkness fascinated her, for they represented a dark energy in him that she wanted, not to know, but to capture for herself, to control—to convert, in her word, to ends that she could smile upon in the open daylight. She was a spirited woman, in her way, and she had her claims to make. Without saying yes or no, she managed to convey to him that, if he did come, he would be expected to live up to higher marks than he usually did. It was another teasing chastisement, baited with smiles that were hesitating and uncertain, perhaps bewildered, perhaps a little frightened.

That was the pattern of their courtship. He would return to her again and again in all the audacity of his desire and pride—to be welcomed on the condition that he become better than he was. He was an ardent and a reckless lover. After she returned to her home, ten miles down the river, almost to Hargrave, he would make that trip two or three times a week, sacrificing his rest to save his work. She shone before him in those days; when he turned his mind to her he saw nothing else. One Sunday afternoon he went to see her, driving a half-broke three-year-old to a buckboard. Seeing her standing on the porch as he drove up, he leapt down and ran up the walk and held her in a long embrace—while behind him the colt was running off, tearing up buckboard and harness and all. She laughed at him, and yet her laughter, even while it exulted in him, refused him as he was. "Oh, Jack," she said, "*look* at you!"

She took to lecturing him, in a way that he loved to indulge and humor, on the sort of prosperous, churchly, respectable man she wanted him to be. That was the curious, nearly obsessive fantasy of their courtship: the sort of man that she would have him become. It delighted him to be thought worthy of her redemption; he half believed in it himself. And all the time he had before him her eyes, her innocent beautiful eyes, and the wonder it would be when they acknowledged his desire.

He won her with his vices, she accepted him as a sort of "mission field," and it was the great disaster of both their lives. He bound her to him by disavowing the very energy that bound him to her. She was bound to him by a vision of him that she held above him—that he, in fact, neither understood nor aspired to; and he was bound to her by a vision of her that she would discover, by her own lights, to be beneath her. Her ambition would be forever as strange and estranging to him as the great heat and strength of his desire would be to her. It is a cruel thing for him now, looking back, to see the two of them working out the terms of their agony. He was a fool—a simpleton and a fool—to have loved so to see the extravagance and grace of his youth reflected in a woman's gray eyes, not by straightforward love or desire, but by what he now knows to have been fear—fear of what she even then instinctively knew to be her opposite, even her enemy. She accepted him as no doubt Saint Paul would have had her accept him—as a challenge to her hope and to her will.

They were extraordinary people, those two. Had it not been so, had they not been so evenly matched, their contest—for that is what it was— might have ended short of marriage. As it was, it had to go on, it had to accept the terms of a final defeat for them both.

Jack was near enough out of debt that he felt he could ask her to marry him. He had a little extra cash that he had laid by. He spent that, and even borrowed a little more, to paint the old house and make the place presentable and cheerful ahead of his wedding day. With the help of Aunt Ren and Uncle Henry, he cleaned the house from top to bottom, opened and aired the disused rooms, let in the light and the wind. They unpacked and washed and returned to the sideboard and the cupboard in the dining room the silver and china that had been his grandmother's. It was an uproarious time they had of it, the three of them—Jack playing as largely as he was able the part of the nervous bridegroom ignorant of the refinements of feminine taste, burlesquing what were, often enough, his real dilemmas, and Aunt Ren and Uncle Henry taking the part of those who knew but, for reasons that he would understand later, chose not to say.

Unwrapping china in the back room upstairs, they came upon his grandfather's ornate chamber pot.

"Now *that's* a beautiful dish, Aunt Ren," Jack said. "I can just see that full of soup."

"*Pore* little thing," Aunt Ren would say. "*Pore* little yellow-headed thing."

And Uncle Henry would laugh until the tears ran down and dripped off his nose.

"So it gets to be nighttime, Uncle Henry, and you take her and you go up to the bedroom and you get undressed and you get in bed, I know about that. *Then* what do you do?"

He was carrying on partly to make them laugh, but mainly because delight was in him and he could not contain it. He was preparing himself and all that he had to be given to Ruth in return only for herself. He felt opening in him the depths of a generosity that he had never known. As their preparations advanced, he would walk through the house alone at night, looking at what they had done, imagining the coming of Ruth, imagining her approval. Once they were married, he thought, once he had brought her here and delivered his place and his life as fully into her hands as he meant to, then her reticence would go away. It would no longer be a matter of his always reaching toward her, always drawing her to himself, pressing his attentions on her, but she would turn freely to him, open to him, in gratitude, seeing that he gave her everything.

He was wrong from the start and did not know it. The powers that had brought them together, that they had played with, bringing themselves together, had played with them, and they did not know it. The thought of it makes him groan aloud and shake his head. He shakes his head and turns and looks—vision returning to him—up the street through town, as if to see relief coming from that direction. But he cannot turn away. He was misled not by Ruth but by his own desire, so strong for her that it saw possibilities that did not exist, and believed in what it saw. And Ruth—an old tenderness wells in him like a flooding stream choked with wreckage and debris—Ruth too was misled, by him, by his foolish willingness to win her by indulging her misconceptions.

What she hoped for perhaps even she herself was not sure. It is only certain that she had not hoped for what she got. Nothing in her experience had prepared her to recognize—much less to value—such a man as Jack Beechum was. Years before, her father had opened a hardware business in town, leaving the work of his farm to a succession of tenants and hired hands. The business did not prosper—it would not until he died and left it to his sons—and neither, in the circumstances, did the farm. At any rate, before Ruth was born her family's ambition had already turned away from the land of its home place toward the business of the town of Hargrave, following the myth of impending prosperity that hovered there over the meeting of the two rivers. But what the town was actually waiting on for prosperity was not the boat traffic of the Kentucky and the Ohio; whether it knew it or not, it was already dependent upon the railroad—and the railroad, when it came, missed the town by several miles.

Their business nevertheless seemed to them to promise ease and wealth such as they could not expect from farming, and once the Lightwoods had turned to the town they did not turn back. Living just beyond the outskirts, they became, in effect, town people. The country bounty of kitchen and garden and orchard and smokehouse served to entertain guests from town: merchants and professional men and the bright young ministers of the various churches. And so when he became her suitor and then her husband, Jack did not exactly occupy a vacancy; he usurped the place of some well-educated young minister or lawyer or doctor whose face and name were perhaps not yet known to the mother and daughter but whose place had nevertheless been appointed. It was this hypothetical and shadowy figure that she held up to Jack as a standard.

He was not a man who could be much dreamed upon; he lived too close to the ground for that. The illusions and false hopes of their courtship could not survive the intimacy of their marriage, and in the failure of their courtship their marriage failed. From the ignorant pleasures of her maidenhood she was transformed on her bridal night to the martyrdom of sexual sainthood. That was as far as it went. That was as far as it was going to go—though he would be years giving up.

There was no joyful arrival, no grateful acceptance of his place and himself and his preparations for her coming. Once the wedding and the festivities were over and they drove away from the crowd of well-wishers at her father's house, together at last outside the bounds of convention and ceremony, there was only a terrible nakedness, in which they saw, before the buggy had gone two miles along the dirt road that led them to the remote place that she had chosen for life, that they were strangers to each other, that they did not know each other at all.

"I hope you'll like the house," he said, suddenly uneasy, seeing it, as he felt she would see it, for the first time, from a distance.

"Oh, I'm sure I will," she said. "I'll like it because it's yours."

But she was watching him. She was withdrawn from him. He felt it, and felt the awareness of what he had done begin to quake in him.

"But it's yours," he said. "You can't like it just to be polite."

She said nothing, and he drove perhaps half a mile before he could bring himself to speak again.

"Wait till you see it. Me and Aunt Ren and Uncle Henry, we fixed it up."

When they drove up to the house he helped her down and loaded himself with her baggage and led the way into the house. The sun was down; the old house, silent as if they were not there, was full of edgeless shadows and the smell of the emptiness of the rooms long unlived in. He felt her sudden desolation. He set down his load and opened a door off the hallway at the foot of the stairs.

"Here's the living room. I've got to take care of the horse. I'll be right back. You make yourself at home."

When he came from the barn a few minutes later and stepped in through the kitchen door, she was sitting in a chair she had drawn away from the table on which Aunt Ren had left their wedding supper overspread with a cloth. She was looking down across the open field into the woods. It was a long warm still evening of late spring. The spell of it was on him, and he came in quietly, stopping just inside the door. For a time, while he stood there, she did not move. And then she stood and turned and walked toward him, but not looking at him, as if she followed some vague instruction.

"Did you look around? Is it all right?"

She nodded. "It's fine."

But she did not look at him. And when he reached out to her and drew her to him and held her, she did not look at him.

A year and a half later, when he sold his crop and returned and laid the canceled mortgage in her hand, it was the same. He wanted her to rejoice, to turn and touch him in her gladness. And he knew that she knew his need. But she could not. Knowing what he wanted, she could not look at him.

By then he knew that she stood in some moral fear of him. He had come to recognize her fear and to feel it. He knew that the touch of his hands had become repugnant to her, and he knew why. His hands were not fastidious, and she had learned their ways, their willingness to do whatever was necessary, to grasp whatever hold was offered, to castrate and slaughter animals, to compel obedience from horse or mule, to cover themselves with whatever filth or dirt or blood his life required. His hands did not hesitate and they did not coax. They did willingly and even eagerly what, before, she had seen only black hands do reluctantly. He had chosen necessities that she had believed a man could come to only by compulsion. That he should touch her, that he should lay his hands on her, as flatly, as openly, with as eager delight, as he laid them on whatever else it delighted him to touch, she could not bear. Under his hand her flesh contracted. He could feel it, her flesh drawing away beneath his hand. He was overpowering to her. His body bent above her in the dark was like a forest at night, full of vast spaces and shadows and the distant outcries of creatures whose names she did not know. He was a strange country and a loneliness to her. And she was doubly lonely because he feared nothing; so deeply did he belong to the place he had brought her to that even its solitude was not lonely to him.

He was intact, sustained within a tradition that she had renounced, or that had been renounced for her before her birth—the yeoman's tradition of sufficiency to himself, of faithfulness to his place. That he was comfortable within the conditions of his life, that he was, in consequence, utterly direct, without disguise or euphemism, in the face of his necessities, made him strange to her. He did not notice that his work clothes stank of manure and horse sweat and his own sweat. She was dismayed to discover that in summer he went without socks and that in winter he slept in his shirt. She spoke of these things, correcting him, and so far as he was able he did as she asked. He studied her wants and fulfilled them as best he could. But he was too thoroughly and deeply formed in himself to change except by deference that rose not out of his desire for her but out of his disappointment. And the deference, even, became always shallower and more perfunctory, for, unable to disguise her estrangement from him and her disapproval of his rough ways, she was forcing him to cease to be simply what he was, and to become defiantly so.

She had the fierce ideological integrity of her ambition. She had the closely ordered calm of her household and her ways. And Jack threatened both with his wildness, his love of ranging in the dark, which she did not feel or understand and so feared. She could not accompany him into the dark. She could not release herself into what she did not know and could not see or foresee. It was not so much that he violated her as that he asked her to violate herself: his rough hand reaching into her bodice, or insinuating itself upon the inside of her thigh, his eye that watched, first gaily and then fearfully, for her response to his hand—they asked her to be broken, to desire what she could not provide, to open herself to a completion of which she would be ever afterward a fragment. And so, though his hand went its way, though he sought the clefts and shelters of her flesh, though he entered her with the awe of a pilgrim, though he drove into her like the taker of a city, though the storm of his desire cast him ashore upon her at last, as meek and strengthless as a child asleep, yet there remained some prize, some vital gift that she withheld. She hid her eyes from him. As much as before their marriage, she remained to him an unknown continent. She offered him no welcome, afforded him no prepared ways. Each time he made his way to her, he came upon her as if by chance, a newcomer, blundering in the dark. He returned each time more fearfully, and at greater expense.

Held by him, overtaken and held in the delayed and violent gusts of his desire, she felt betrayed, victimized; it seemed to her that the roof and walls of the old house fell away, exposing her to the stars and the dark distances. It seemed to her that she was not there at all, but alone, lost, exiled in a dark wilderness whose trees she was afraid even to lift her hands to touch. And she would be deeply still then, in fear of being overheard by whatever followed, hearing the wind and the distant cries. He was her cross, and she bore him with a submission that, afterwards, chilled him to the bone. They lay beside each other in solitude, as rigid and open-eyed as effigies.

And so it seemed to Jack a continuation of a misery already begun and familiar when he stood, drenched with her cries, to receive into his hands the shrouded body of the only son they would have, dead.

Four : Will Wells

"What's the matter, old friend?"

"Who's that?"

"Are you all right?"

Now there is a hand on his shoulder, friendly, careful of him.

"I'm all right. I thank you, Irvin."

And now that he is paying attention again, he sees that it is Jayber Crow.

"I thank you, Jayber. How are you, son?"

"I'm fine. I thought a minute ago you didn't sound all right."

And now Old Jack remembers the sound of his outcry, and feels the coolness of tears on his face.

"Ah," he says, "ay Lord," ashamed to have made a fuss, not having meant to.

Jayber is standing in front of him now, watching him. Everything about Jayber is long—body, legs and arms, hands, face, nose. He is all a morose, downward-hanging length, except for his mouth, which is customarily turned up like a saucer in a lean, boyish smile. And his eyes—his eyes are large and brown and round, full of little glistenings and foretokenings of humor. The men who know him will always remember him in profile, that alert brown eye watching from its vantage in the long face like a squirrel looking out of a hole in a tree. Just now he has his barber's comb stuck over his ear. And he is smiling at Old Jack, beginning to believe that he is indeed all right.

"Why don't you come in and sit down a while?"

Old Jack nods, and Jayber leads him to the door and up the step into the barbershop.

"Right over here now. See if that chair won't fit you," Jayber says, guiding him toward the back of the room, to what he considers the best of his mixed collection of chairs.

With Jayber's help, Old Jack lets himself down.

"Ah!" he says, glad to be off his feet.

Besides himself and Jayber the shop is occupied at present by a fat young woman with three little boys getting their hair cut in preparation for the start of school.

The shop settles down now and Old Jack settles with it. He can smell the mixed smells of talcum and lotion and soap. The burner on which Jayber heats his shaving water whispers busily, and there is the rhythmic snick-snick of Jayber's scissors. The barber's face has taken on the bemusement of his work. Old Jack recognizes the mood and takes comfort. Eased again of the present, his mind resumes its task: to come through, to survive yet again its old trial.

The stillbirth of their son does not bring them together, as in the first moments he desperately hoped that it might. He has little more than stepped over the threshold into the room where Ruth lies when he understands that it will not. Aunt Ren and the doctor have gone out to the kitchen. The hard brightness of winter dawn, sunlight on snow, has filled the room. It is deeply still, the enormous quiet of the cold day reaching inside to meet an answering quiet that seems to him as great. Both he and Ruth seem to be held, suspended, in a palpable silence whose pressure he can feel in his chest and throat. He goes and stands at the foot of the bed. Ruth lies straight and still, her body as formally composed as a corpse, her eyes shut. He knows that she knows he has come in, but she does not open her eyes. Her eyelids are seals upon the stillness. For what seems to him a long time he stands there, unable to speak or move, aware of his intrusiveness, his solitude, as a man might be who stands alone on the horizon of a treeless plain of snow. And then he makes a business of building up the fire, and goes out. He has the cold wind to face. He has his stock to feed, drinking holes to chop in the ice of the ponds.

If she had acknowledged then a need that he could have answered, it might have changed, might have been different. Or it might have been different—as he has thought many times since her death—if he had had the grace or the forbearance to have gentled and humbled himself then, while he was still there in the room with her. If he had just sat down in a chair beside her and waited, maybe finally he would have been able to offer something that she needed. In the seventeen years that Ruth has been dead his mind has gone back again and again to that moment, pondering over it as one might ponder over the dead, dry bud of a flower, sensing beyond it, lost in it, the possibility of a gentle and welcoming efflorescence that, had there been some mysterious difference, might have opened toward him. What if he had been a gentler, humbler man? What if their son had lived? Through all the years he has never lost his first vision of her, and never ceased to mourn the descent of that vision into the diminished reality that he knows he helped to make, though he has never understood exactly how. Was it his pride, his defiance of her attempts to change him, his silence for want of grace or humility when he stood that February morning at the foot of her bed? Whether it might have changed anything or not, he should have sat down beside her and waited.

He could not. He did not. His own pride and pain were too great. He had already too many times been driven to her as a supplicant by an unconquerable need for her, who acknowledged no need for him. As his suffering was so much less respectable than hers who had borne the child, he carried it off in himself and said nothing. However he mended it over with the skin of silence, it festered in his depths and grew.

After that birth the house again became for him a place of sorrow and failure, as it had been during his childhood. Again he sought his comfort in the fields. But now he was seeking for it with a man's need and a man's desperation, and he found little enough. He was working hard, making his days longer than ever, saving some money, for what he did not yet quite know. But his workdays no longer had the order and clarity that he had known in them before. Now it was as though his bafflement stretched like an opaque membrane between him and the sky, and he was darkened. He went to his fields nevertheless with the sense that he belonged to them more than he belonged to the house. Before, between him and

Ruth, there had been the strain of pretense that all was as it should be—a strain that nevertheless had permitted her to attempt to correct him, and him either to comply or to resist. Now there was silence between them. And as the weight of what was unacknowledged grew, it became a silence that he was less and less able to bear.

In all outward things Ruth was a good wife. Since their marriage, she had gradually changed the house, so that now, with the help of the odds and ends of money that he encouraged her to put into it, it was better cared for and more comfortable than he had ever known it. Aunt Ren had continued to come to the house to work as before, but she was failing now and most of the work fell to Ruth, the old woman serving as a self-appointed teacher and companion, puttering at what suited her, talking indiscriminately to Ruth or to herself. Ruth cooked and washed and cleaned and sewed and canned and preserved and looked after her chickens and turkeys and, except for the plowing, kept the garden. She went faithfully to the church—more and more frequently she went alone—and became a member of the Missionary Society. And in all this she made a life for herself that, though it served and even pleased him, was different and remote from his life. Surrounded and contained by this life of hers, she seemed happy, even serene. He loved and suffered from the glimpses he caught of her bent over her sewing, or at work in the garden, unaware of him. Then her face would be eased and lovely, in absentness of concentration, unresisting. His entrances broke the gentle surrounding of this life, and then her silence would become a withholding. The set of her face would change. Her beauty had become a ghost to him; it vanished from his direct vision as from his touch. His presence was an invasion, a violation of the house. And except to eat and sleep, he began to stay away.

Now, instead of going into the living room or out on the porch after supper to sit until bedtime, he went back to the barn, if the weather permitted, and kept himself busy there until dark. Or he would sit, resting, on an upturned bucket in the open doorway, his horses and mules feeding and stirring quietly in their stalls behind him. On wet days he would work at the barn, or rest there, or he would walk the fences and the boundaries of the farm, his feet and hands as restless as his mind.

He was no longer thinking about the possibilities of his own place that had once so held and exalted his mind. Unrealized as many of them remained, they no longer seemed to be enough. He no longer seemed to himself to be enough. He knew that he had been found wanting in Ruth's eyes, which meant, since her eyes had become the only qualification of his, that he was now found wanting in his own. Her judgment of him, however he might have resented and defied it, had entered into him, and her judgment was that though he might have pride and desire, growing out of his sense of himself and his place, he had, properly speaking, no ambition. He did not want to improve himself or enrich himself or come up in the world. He was a limited man, and offensively so insofar as he appeared satisfied within his limits. And so he began to move now, as he thought, in defiance of her judgment, but actually in unconscious obedience to her judgment's chief implication: that no place may be sufficient to itself, but must lead to another place, and that all places must finally lead to money; that a man's work must lead not to the health of his family and the respect of his neighbors but to the market place, to that deference that strangers yield to sufficient cash.

What he had in his mind now as he sat and thought, or walked the lengths of afternoons and thought, or worked and thought, was more land. He wanted more land. A man falling in his own esteem needs more ground under his feet; to stand again he may need the whole world for a foothold. His thoughts now ranged over the resources within his boundaries, and over the possibilities that lay outside them, seeking the terms of some new balance. His mind played over and over again the airy drama of ambition: how to use what he had to get what he wanted—a strange and difficult undertaking for him, who until then had wanted only what he had. Once he had hungered for the life his place could be made to yield. Now he would ask it to yield another place, at what expense to itself and to him he could not then have guessed.

The current of his thoughts had now resurrected, without consciousness of its source, one of the fantasies that Ruth had persistently woven about their courtship and that he had indulged at that time: the idea that the two of them would better themselves, that he would become a great landowner, that they would have the respect of the best people who knew them, that they would send their children to the best schools and see them started in careers that would make them even more wealthy and respected than their parents. He had once taken this merely as an extravagant compliment to himself, very pleasing, since he reckoned without much thinking about it that he more or less deserved it. Now he turned to it desperately, as to a last hope.

It happened at that time that the farm known as the Farrier place, adjoining his, was about to be offered for sale. The main stem of the family that had owned it had died out, and the heirs were scattered. While they had bickered over the settlement of the estate, the place had been rented to Sims McGrother, a neighbor on the other side, who had subjected it to a good deal of abuse and neglect. The old Farrier house had burned down in the year after its abandonment, leaving its two stone chimneys standing, the fireplaces opening blankly into the daylight once enclosed by the log rooms. Yard and garden had grown up in weeds and bushes, shutting off the house's outlook on its fields. It was on this place that Jack's restless thoughts and hopes now came to earth and took form.

The farm was not large—something less than a hundred acres. It was generally steeper and rougher than his land, and he knew the weakness of its south slopes that lay along the West Fork facing his good north ones. But half of it was ridge land that could be mended and made good. That the house was gone was not a great disadvantage to him, who would not be living there, and the other buildings were good, as were the fences. A number of times he walked over it, looking at it, loosening the earth in the rows of the crop ground with his heel, picking it up and crumbling it in his fingers. He examined through a whole summer the quality of the growth in all the fields. He drank from the well and the spring and lingered by the waterholes along the creek. He looked at the foundation and the framing and the roof of every one of the buildings.

He was learning a new desire, the subtlety and power of which surprised him. Like the "strange woman" whose delights were so carefully understood by Solomon, this new place claimed an ample space in his mind, which it implanted with its impulse and will, and filled with visions. It possessed as much of his consciousness as might stray from his work; it kept him awake at night. He wanted to see that place respond to him. He wanted to see it dress itself in green and be fertile and abundant for his sake. Before long there was not a building or a field inside the Farrier line that was not invested with a plan or a vision that bore the by then unmistakable mark of the character and the ways of Jack Beechum. They were the good and saving ways that had doubled the health and the abundance of his own place in the years since his father's death.

One hot day late in the summer he ate his dinner and went out and sat down in the doorway of the barn, giving his mules time to rest before starting back to the field. Sitting there, he began to think of the Farrier place, and on an impulse saddled his horse and rode down to the line fence. He hitched his horse in the shade and crossed the dry bed of the creek and climbed slowly up through the heavy heat of the little valley onto the Farrier ridge. He crossed a tobacco patch, walking between two rows, and stopped in the shade of a big walnut tree that stood just beyond the row ends. He was high up and could see along the ridge ahead of him to the chimneys of the burned house and, beyond, to where its lane started down the bluff to the creek. And back the way he had come he could see over the ridge tops of his own place to his house and barns. All around the distances were blue in the heat haze. The ridges stood open to the sun above the woods, and everywhere in the downward leaning of the slopes was the intimation of shade along the streams— deep shade, and here and there the still gleam of a pool of water, or the constant small splashing of a spring.

For some time he stood and looked. It was the first time he had come here on a workday, and it was a difference that he felt strongly. To come when he had no work to do might require an interest that was little more than idle; no matter how elaborate and ardent had been his visions, they need not possess him, they could be discarded, so long as he offered them only his idle time. That he was there when he had good reason not to be, when he could have been at work in his own fields—that was a serious declaration, and he knew it. He said to himself very deliberately then what he found himself relieved and even eager to say: that if there was any way to do it, when the place was sold, he would buy it. He said that to himself and then a shudder shook him, for he knew he would do as he said.

He was about to start home when he saw a stain of dust rising into the haze above the rim of the bluff, and when he listened he could hear a wagon's wheels beating over the stones and ledges of the lane. And then almost at once the team and wagon came in sight. He knew it would be Sims McGrother. His first thought was to keep from being seen. There was a wooded draw not far from where he stood; once in the cover of the draw he could have gone on down to the creek and back to where he had left his horse without having to come into the open again. But though his whole body tensed with his wish to be gone, he did not move. He did not want to be seen slipping away. He did not want to know that he had slipped away. And he particularly did not want to be moved by Sims McGrother.

Jack did not like McGrother, who was a big talker and a waster. With his two sons and several families of Negroes, McGrother farmed a tract of six hundred acres adjoining the Farrier place on two sides and going all the way to the river. It had been good land, but under McGrother's use it had declined. McGrother was hard on himself and on his men and on everything he touched—a roughness that he loved to brag about as if it were no more than honest plainness and a devotion to hard work. His hands would with equal indifference ruin a horse's mouth or a hillside. He loved to handle cash, and he drove himself and all that belonged to him in the direction of money as if it were as far off as heaven and as if he were running out of time; but he also loved his own driving and his roughness, and he loved to speak of it. "Kill a mule, buy another'n, kill a nigger, hire another'n," he would say. His women hung behind him, out of his reach, watchful of his wrath, as anxious and fluttery as killdees. His abuse of other things always involved abuse of himself. In his fifties then, he was in appearance a characteristic product of his own making; worn lean and ragged, his face, within its nap of gray beard, burnt and wrinkled and dry. Three fingers of his left hand had been cut off above the third joint, leaving the thumb and forefinger a kind of double claw.

Jack rather expected that he would go to the barn, since there was little reason at that time for him to be coming to the tobacco patch in a wagon. But McGrother came on past the barn. He was driving what Jack recognized as a typical McGrother team: a pair of mules with the hair rough on them and their ribs showing, mismatched in size and color, unsheared, overworked.

McGrother whips the team into a trot, and they come on back the

ridge straight toward Jack, the dust flying from under the wheels and the
bolsters pounding. And he comes on, letting the mules slow to a walk,
and stops them in front of Jack, the tongue almost touching him.

"Whoa!"

"Howdy," Jack says.

"Howdy."

McGrother, sitting on a plank that lies across the sideboards of the
wagon bed, leans forward, elbows on his knees, check lines dangling from
his hands, and looks at Jack as if he is something inanimate, a post or a
tree, that cannot look back. The sight of the worn-out, ill-used team has
already filled Jack with contempt and pity, and now this blatant stare of
McGrother's makes him furious. But he only stands without moving, as
if he is indeed a post or a tree that McGrother will have either to run over
or back up and drive around. For some seconds neither of them says
anything, their locked stares drawn between the two mules as rigidly as
the wagon tongue.

"Well, how do you like it?" McGrother says.

"I like it all right."

"By God, I reckon you do. You been over here enough." McGrother
grins and nods. "I've seen your tracks."

Jack goes around the lead mule to stand by the left front wheel of the
wagon. He is within arm's reach of McGrother now. "I left them to be
seen. I never tried to hide them." Close as he is to McGrother now, he
can feel anger tightening his throat. The desire to take hold of McGrother
is as pressing in him as hunger.

"But you ain't bought it yet." McGrother grins, looking down at him.
He shakes once with laughter. "It ain't yours yet, not by a damn sight.
And if you beat me to it you'll have to get up before day."

"Then I'll get up before day," Jack says.

His hands want to get hold of McGrother and pull him down out of
the wagon. But that would not do and he knows it. He knows what it
would mean to have that behind him and the consequences of it ahead
of him. He is afraid McGrother will say something else, but he cannot
leave or move or look away yet. He stands a long moment, giving
McGrother his chance, and then walks away. He does not look back, and
he is a long time in the open, going down the ridge. It is not until he has

gone in among the trees on the bluff that he hears the wagon move. He stands and listens as it turns and goes back to the barn. And then he goes on down through the trees, through the briary patch of hillside pasture, across the creek, and over the rock fence to where his horse is standing.

He went back to the barn and hitched up his mules and worked through the afternoon. But now he was changed. The Farrier place had changed him. His trip over there that day had formalized a sort of betrothal; it had joined his vision to his will. Now his desire was no longer a dream; it was an intention, and McGrother's presence had forced him to declare it aloud. His vision of the redemption of that place was, he now realized, an investment in it. The thought of its possible loss increased his desire. It was a desire that would have carried him across the sea in a wooden ship, or through the Cumberland Gap on foot, or on horseback across the desert, had he not been too much a farmer ever to yearn so far beyond the ground under his feet. What he sought was not the unknown of distance, but the unknown of time: the yearly unfolding of the flower and fruit of the land he knew. And now, having allowed that desire to reach out beyond his own boundaries, he felt its exposure; he must rescue and preserve it and secure its triumph. He could not bear the thought that McGrother might circumvent him. Though the times were hard he would take the gamble. It was well that he had already done his thinking, for now was the time of his passion.

He had a principle against interrupting his workdays; having already interrupted this one once, he finished it at the usual time. But after supper that night he saddled his horse and rode to Hargrave. He hunted out the house of the lawyer he knew to be handling the Farrier estate and offered for the farm a figure that he thought would be higher than McGrother would offer. The lawyer gladly received the bid and agreed that Jack would not be named as the bidder and that he would be notified if the bid was raised. Having had his part of the conversation well rehearsed, Jack was at leisure to watch the lawyer's face, and he rode home confident that his bid had been the first and also unexpectedly high. He got home after midnight. "Well, I'm up before day," he thought. "And I didn't tell him how far before day it would be."

Now he needed time, and it happened that he had plenty. The Farrier place was not offered for sale until the February of the next year. Meantime Jack never went near it. He did not speak of what he had done or of what he hoped. He did not tell Ruth or Ben or Nancy or anyone except the lawyer, who was evidently as good as his word. When he met McGrother, and occasionally he went out of his way to do that, he spoke and held himself as if their meeting at McGrother's tobacco patch had never occurred. He watched McGrother's face, and he knew McGrother did not know. He was solitary in those days, keeping his own counsel, saying little, watching. At times he felt the exultant secrecy of a man waiting in ambush. He had made the possibility and seen the vision of his new desire, and he alone knew what it was.

He knew when the lawyer finally offered the farm for sale. And from that time his attention never left McGrother. He was as ardent now in his cunning as he had ever been in love. He knew the times when McGrother was likely to be in town, and he was there when McGrother was. He made occasions to travel the river road past McGrother's house. It was the first time in his life—and it was to be the last—that he ever resorted to stealth and deception, but he was pleased, for a while he was pleased, to discover that he was good at it. From the covert of his own apparent good humor and disinterest, as though he moved, faded in among the trees, along the edges of the other man's life, he watched. So intently did he watch that all that he saw was plain to him. He knew almost to the hour when McGrother made his bid, and knew from the change in McGrother's face that it had been low and that McGrother was thinking it over. He knew that McGrother was watching *him* now, baffled: if Jack had not made the high bid, then who had? Who else wanted the place? But as though he was always facing away from what he had most on his mind, he revealed nothing. He went quietly to the bank and arranged, provisionally, to borrow the money he would need. All that he did now was deliberate and well foreseen. He delighted in the deepening revelations of this cunning that he had not known he possessed. When he met McGrother or his sons he would talk as long as they would, allowing the conversation to go where it might, never batting an eye when they deliberately spoke, testing him, of the Farrier place and of the desirability of buying land and of its value. And then he would turn and walk away, not turning his head, knowing that they watched him as long as he was in sight.

As it drew on toward March he began to feel the strain. If the Farrier place was to be his he needed to be making his plans, and he needed to see about hiring some help. He was keeping that *if* steadily in mind. And then he got word that his bid had been accepted. He rode to Hargrave and signed deed and mortgage, and felt the past close behind him and the future open. He was in the clear. Or so he thought.

Riding home, instead of going on to his own place, he turns into the lane that climbs the hill to the Farrier place. He is the owner now, and he will not enter it the first time as owner by coming in over the back fence as he has done before. Now he will ride in through the front gate. He goes eagerly up the narrow lane, rising through the trees, coming out finally onto the open ridge.

McGrother is there ahead of him this time. He is at the barn, loading onto his wagon the few tools he has left there. He turns and looks as Jack's horse stops in the door. For a second they say nothing, as if to allow all the implications of this meeting to assemble.

"You," McGrother says. And then he breathes deliberately, as if that is something he has been neglecting to do.

"Me," Jack says.

He rides back the ridge and down to the creek. When he reaches the boundary he tears down enough of the rock fence to make a gate. He rides through.

Laughter gathers in the air around him, surprising him. He did not expect it there in the gray February evening between the leafless slopes of the hollow, and he reins in his horse and looks around. The years flow past him, but still for some seconds the times overlap and he seems to be sitting on horseback though he is in the barbershop. And now, as though gently sinking, he comes to himself again in his chair, no reins in his hands but only the crook of his cane, though even in his reverie he has kept as straight in his seat as a rider. Now the woman and the three little boys are gone, and in their place are three or four of the loafers, to whose talk Jayber is listening, having now climbed into the barber chair himself. The heavy chair holds him somewhat higher than the others; he leans back, at ease, Olympian, his eye lit with amusement and anticipation.

To Old Jack it is as though he has slept through a change of season. He is still and he slowly becomes aware of his stillness. And now his hands twitch and waken where they rest on the crook of the cane, and he moves one of them to the edge of his chair. He gets up, rising against stiffness as under a burden, and makes his way out the back door. He relieves himself and then stands, smelling dinner cooking somewhere, suddenly hungry. He looks at his watch. Twenty after ten. At Mat's, in the tobacco patch, they will soon be dividing the crew, some to keep on cutting, some to start loading so they can bring loaded wagons to the barn when they come in to dinner. He knows in his flesh the old relief they feel now, having come to the downslope of the morning, dinner ahead of them, before the long pull of the afternoon.

He returns to the shop and sits down again. From his height Jayber is watching him, but Old Jack does not know that. He has composed himself, hands on his cane, head tilted back a little, mouth open, gazing sightlessly at the wall. A deep quiet has drawn around him again, as though the front of the shop, where the talkers are, has simply moved away. In his quiet he is aware of another name ahead of him, to be raised up again in its old flesh and given voice: Will Wells.

For in buying the Farrier place he had destroyed his old independence. He had more to do now than he could do alone. Uncle Henry was still there, of course, as he would be until he died. But Uncle Henry had already been old a long time and he would not be able for long to do the little that he still did. Jack needed a good hand, and after some looking around he hired a young Negro man who had been recommended to him by Perry Clemmons. This was a strongly built dark man, whose eyes had a straight, calm look that Jack liked. He had a wife, Marthy, lighter in color than himself, and four children. He was said to be a good worker, a quiet man, one who could be depended on. His name was Will Wells.

There was on the Farrier place a small house of two rooms, long disused, and this they repaired for Will and his family, who moved in at the end of the second week of March. Will lived up to the good that had been said of him, and more. He would get out early and stay late. He would work responsibly alone. He took an intelligent pride in what he did, and was able to see what needed to be done and to do it without being told. He was a good man with stock and a competent teamster. He was perhaps four or five years younger than Jack, strong, proud of his strength, eager in its use.

There grew between the two of them a relationship—a sort of broth-erhood—of an intensity that Jack would know only that once. Though they assumed the inevitable economic roles of master and servant, they were from the beginning equals before the work. It would not have occurred to Jack to ask another man to do a job that he would not do himself, or to hold back while another man took the hardest part, or to rest while another man worked. That was his principle and his pride. Though Will worked for Jack's benefit, he did not work for his conven-ience. That they worked side by side, that they knew the same hardships of labor and weather, made a ground of respect between them, and a liking. They teamed together as if they had been born twins. Both were big men, both strong, both liked the work. And in the time they were together they did an amount of it that amazed both themselves and the men who knew them. They acquired a local fame as a team among the farmers who worked with them in the tobacco setting and in the har-vest. When the two of them stepped up, other men stood back.

Little idle talk ever passed between them. They might work closely together for half a day without speaking, cooperating like the two hands of a single body, anticipating each other's moves like partners in a dance. They did not speak of their lives. They met and did their work and parted and went their ways. They met in Port William as awkwardly as strangers. It was in the work itself, not in anything that the work came from or led to, that they made the terms and the comfort of their com-radeship. At times in the heat and striving of some hard day their eyes would meet and acknowledge the strange grace of their labor.

In two years they set the Farrier place to rights with the same assured sense of order with which a housewife would have tidied a room. They repaired the fences and cleared the bushes and briars from the neglected pastures and removed the clutter that had accumulated in and around the buildings. The boundaries and edges became clear. There remained a number of jobs that waited on money, such as repairing and painting the buildings, and there remained the slow healing of the abused and weakened ground. But the healing had been begun. After the ragged idle-ness of neglect, the encroachment of thicket upon its cleared ground, the old place had resumed a kind of repose within its human limits. The daylight, falling on it, received an order from it that Jack loved to recognize as his own. And he was making it pay. At the end of two years he was beginning to see his way out.

There began now to be a new adjustment between him and Ruth. Though he had not spoken to her of his plans, they had become plain enough. She believed she saw a direction in them that promised her some sort of deliverance. Once the new place was paid for they would buy another one, for that was the logic of the process, and after that, no doubt, another one. They would hire more men to do the work. She began to have a vision of Jack as a man on horseback, overseeing the work of other men. Perhaps later they would move to town. Perhaps they would travel. The money hunger of her father and brothers had represented itself to her in a Sunday version that had encouraged her own longing for a refinement protected by the labor of servants and the scruples of "gentlemen." She did not exactly know what she wanted, any more than she knew what Jack's expansionist efforts might make of him. But she found relief and even attraction in her new sense of him as a man redefining himself, for it had been her realization of him as a man defined that had caused her unhappiness. She began to see herself again when she looked in her mirror—a woman whose beauty had perhaps not yet done all its work. She would lead him into a better life. Guardedly, she turned toward him again. She became pregnant with her second child.

And Will Wells had begun the makings of a life on the Farrier place that belonged to it much more particularly than Jack's ever would. Working at odd times, mostly alone, but with Jack's help when he needed it, Will had elaborated around his little house the design of a neat homestead. Little by little he had fixed up the henhouse and had fenced the boundaries of yard and garden and hogpen. He had built a pen and coops for his chickens, and had re-laid the flagstones and the stone steps leading to the front door. Although Jack never set foot in the house, he saw the order around it and saw that Marthy raised a good garden and had flowers in the yard. By the terms of their agreement, Will was given three meat hogs a year and the use of a milk cow. And the team of mules he worked he stabled and fed in the barn on the Farrier place. Except that it was not his place, except that he had to hold himself answerable to Jack, he was at home there. And as long as he was satisfied to satisfy

Jack, that was a difference that did not have to be made or observed by either of them. They were getting along. As soon as he could spare the money Jack was going to add a room to the little house and paint it.

Jack saw what Will had done, what a pleasant, frugal order he had made, and he admired it. But he found to his surprise that it troubled him too. In some strange way he feared it. He feared the claim it made on his respect and his feelings. For it was *his* farm; his was the permanent relation there; it was his name on the deed and the mortgage, and his life whose continuance in that place the law anticipated and protected. The small domestic order that Will Wells had made there was almost accidental, a passing fact like a day or a season, its impermanence full of sorrow that Jack recognized by an impulse of sympathy that was deep, for he liked the man. And yet he strove against it because he saw in it the threat of an anguish that would be his own.

This difference between them, though for a while it did not have to be acknowledged, was too great. There came between them in the third year, not an open break, but a disharmony, a withdrawal from the center of their agreement. There began to be a roughening, an imprecision, in their teamwork that made them conscious and resentful of their dependence on each other. To Jack this had become a confinement. He began to fret in the knowledge that, having so much land to farm, he could not move except in relation to the other man. And as if to keep him reminded of this condition, Will's work began to deviate subtly from Jack's directions and expectations. He did not shirk; he just moved aside from the deep consent of their beginning. Now when they worked together there would be some trifling but nevertheless irritating discrepancy of pace or intention. In Will this was the result of a failure of interest that had been immanent all along in his knowledge that his labor formalized and preserved no bond between him and the place; he was a man laboring for no more than his existence. On Jack's side of the difference there was an increasing resentment of his dependence and a jealous remembering of days before he met Ruth, when in his solitary work he had been so free.

One afternoon in the June of that third year, Will Wells started across a hollow in a little swale with a wagonload of hay. It was wetter there from a recent rain than either of them had thought, but nevertheless Will should have avoided the place. The team drew the front wheels across, but then, where the front wheels had cut deeply into the mud, the back wheels sank deeper, and stayed. The team could not move it.

They are on the Farrier place, a long way from another team. It has been hot all day long, the air still and heavy, a weight to be lifted. And all day they have hurried against the return of the rain, loading the wagon in the field in the glare of the hazy sun, unloading it in the smothering dim cave of the barn. At last they are on the downslope of the day—a load loaded, a load left on the ground, the end in sight, and the sky darkening. And now in the very path of their haste stands the massive immobility of the mired wagon. Jack cannot believe it. That the wagon that was moving only minutes ago cannot now be moved is an affront to the logic of his haste. He stands in the mud, covered with chaff, drenched with sweat, furious. It is Will's team but Jack has the reins. He thinks of handing them to Will, but almost in the same instant he calls on the team again and takes hold of a brace at the side of the wagon frame and pulls. The mules tighten willingly, the breast chains clatter, the men strain in silence.

"Whoa."

The mules step back to slacken the traces. Jack stands there, the reins dangling from his hand. He can feel the blood pressing into the veins of his throat. He is looking off into the sky over the heads of the mules, not wanting to look at Will Wells. He feels the imminence of new fate in whatever will happen next, and so even in his fury he pauses. And then he looks at Will.

"Go get a shovel!"

No such words have ever passed between them. Will recognizes the challenge and the accusation in them but he turns and hurries off toward the barn.

Jack drops the reins now. Going to some trees that stand nearby in a fence row, he picks up a heavy fallen branch. With the branch and his hands he begins to dig in front of one of the mired wheels. The rain is closer now. The new energy of his words to Will Wells stays in his mind and gladdens him with the fatalistic joy of his anger. He loosens chunks of wet sod with the branch and then claws them out of the way with his hands, hurrying, throwing himself recklessly into the work, though he knows now that the hay is going to get wet no matter what he does. He is abandoned in his fury; his labor is no longer work, but a striving against the effrontery of circumstance.

Will returns with the shovel and begins to dig beside him. For several seconds they work there, too close together, in each other's way, bumping against each other. And then Jack throws his stick aside and reaches for the shovel. He takes hold of it as if to jerk it out of Will's hands. They straighten up, both holding to the handle. Jack sees Will's eyes ignite, showing their anger to him, refusing to turn loose. "Ah!" Jack thinks. "Ah now!"

For a moment the two of them stand braced against each other's weight like two men poised at the top of a steeple, holding on. And then they are at each other. Neither makes any motion to evade or fend off. They meet in the open embrace of their fury, eager to damage each other, not minding the cost. It is a strange dance they do now, locked in each other's arms, each striving to stand against the other's determination that he will fall. They stagger and grunt with their effort, tramping and stamping to keep their feet under them, leaving their tracks deep in the soft ground.

And then Jack feels suddenly a change in himself. It is the irresistible change of revelation—unexpected, to the end of his life never quite accountable. Locked in that desperate double embrace, he has come aware as never before of the man he is fighting. He feels in his hands the heat and sweat and anguish of the man, Will Wells. He feels the presence of the man, the desire and energy and frustration never contained in the narrow order of their workdays.

Or that must be what it is. Their anger has carried them beyond the prescribed bounds, and for Jack, perhaps because his own grievance is momentary compared with that of the other man, the revelation is quick to come. And it is disarming. Helplessly, he feels his anger leave him. As evenly matched as they are, that makes a critical difference.

Though he still struggles to defend himself, he is losing ground now. He is being backed slowly toward the wagon. And then Will shrugs loose from his hold. Jack sees the right fist cocked in the air, and feels it crash against his temple. Lights scatter around him and he falls, the ground for a long moment seeming to sink away beneath him. Dimly he expects another blow, but no other falls and he lies still. His eyes open and he sees Will Wells walking away toward his house, dejected, covered with chaff and sweat, his shirt torn half off. Still Jack does not get up. In a while he will get up and dig out the buried wheels and throw off some of the load and drive the wagon to the barn. But now he does not move. As he lies there his new vision of Will Wells completes itself. Everything is finished between them, he knows, for the reason that nothing was ever really started. A vast difference lived between them even while they worked together—the difference between hopeful and hopeless work. And now Will is going home to tell Marthy and their children that they will have to leave the place that they have worked and made. Jack feels the sorrow of a man who must always leave whatever he has made that is dear to him, who like a ghost must always leave behind the earth that he knows.

It is final. Their anger was the end of words. Between them now is a silence against which they have no speech. They cannot be reconciled, for no real peace ever existed between them, and they are far off in history from the terms and the vision of such a peace. Jack knows now what it was he asked of Will Wells, and knows he cannot ask it again of another man. And so he lies still, knowing that another of the inexorable hinges of his life has turned. And now on the stubble of the hayfield and over the hollows and ridges and roofs of the countryside, the rain has begun to fall.

For some moments he sits looking out of himself into the barbershop where Jayber listens to the daily installment of the endless conversation of the loafers. But the sound of that rain falling has come out of its time and filled his ears, so that to him the faces of the talkers are silent, and he watches them as through a window. He knows that he will have to turn back again into the old country of his past, for his troubles are upon him now and it is a long way to the end.

That he might have hired another hand to replace Will Wells on the Farrier place was a possibility that he would not allow to enter his mind. Trading work with his neighbors, he struggled on to the end of the year. He marketed his crops. And then, with the new crop year coming on, it became urgent that he find a buyer for the Farrier place, for it was obvious that he could not farm both places without help. He had been quietly looking for a buyer since the time of his fight with Will, trying to keep word of it from McGrother. But he had found no buyer, and now he knew that McGrother was on to him. His dislike had made him too close a student of McGrother for him to miss that. McGrother had found out and now he was watching him, biding his time.

The January of the new year came and on the twenty-fourth Ruth gave birth to their second—and last—child, a daughter, Clara. For months before that, since he had told her of his intention to sell the Farrier place, Jack and Ruth had been more deeply at odds than ever. To Ruth that was the signal of a profound foreclosure on her life: what she was, she was destined to be. At first she controlled her anger and her despair well enough to try to argue with him. She tried to reason with him, referring to her own old dream of the future as if it had been the sole condition of their marriage. But when she saw that he would not be changed, she turned away from him, punishing him with a denial that he now knew would last forever. They would, of course, speak as necessary to each other; as time went on there would be even a sort of respectful friendliness between them, haunted by the lost possibility of which it was the remnant. But they would never have between them the one life of their marriage; in its place there would be a silent and barren and forbidden ground.

And so when he went as before into the bedroom after the departure of the doctor, he went as a man acknowledging a responsibility from which he expects no reward. He went acknowledging himself to have been the cause of a suffering for which he expected no forgiveness.

This time her eyes are open and she is looking at him. He crosses the room and stands as before at the foot of the bed. She shows the exhaustion of her labor, her hair in disarray as she has seldom allowed him to see it, her face pale. But now she has found the strength of her anger and she is looking at him. The baby lies on the bed beside her, hidden from him by a fold of the counterpane.

"I'll not go through this again," she says. "Do you understand?"

He understood. There had already been times when, having no words for her silence, unable to bear it, he had slept alone in the room above the kitchen. He had, in fact, been sleeping there since early in the winter. Now it was confirmed and final. He knew that he would sleep alone the rest of his life. Lying in the bare room whose curtainless windows admitted the bright, implacable gaze of the stars, he knew that he had become the incarnation of his solitude. He bore it in silence and with a bitterness that now began to drive him.

Ruth slept downstairs with the baby. It happened, perhaps because of Ruth's preoccupation with her disappointment and not by intention, but nevertheless it happened that Jack was never shown the baby. Until she learned to come to him on her own he would see her only in accidental encounters and in distant sightings. And that, too, established a pattern that would last. Rarely now did he go deeper into the house than the kitchen and his bedroom above it which he reached by a stairway from the back porch. Aunt Ren, who lay sick all that winter, would die early in the spring. After that there would be only the three of them. The house would become a defensive feminine enclosure to which Jack would have only a peripheral connection.

And so as that winter came to an end, solitude and failure were heavy on his mind. On the first of March, when he went, beaten, to McGrother and accepted the same offer for the Farrier place that McGrother had made three years ago, he was filled with a reckless bitterness and anger. But by his lights, then and now, he had no other choice. He had lost his three years' work. He had sold the Farrier place at a heavy loss. He was still in debt, and for nothing. It was as though the veil of hopelessness that, without his knowing it, had hung over the past three years now darkened the future too. For nothing.

The following Saturday afternoon he rode to Port William to get his horse shod. The blacksmith finished the work and Jack mounted again, but he remained there, sitting on his horse outside the shop door, talking. The shop stood perhaps fifty feet back from the road, leaving a cinder-covered yard in front of it where the blacksmith worked in good weather. The view of the road was blocked on one side by the building in which Jasper Lathrop now has his store and on the other by the hotel.

As Jack is talking with the blacksmith, he hears from up the street in front of the hotel a laugh that he recognizes as McGrother's. And then:

"Hell yes! His place and three years of his and that big nigger's work!"

The laugh comes again.

Jack turns his horse and rides slowly out into the street. McGrother and his sons have just driven into town. The three of them are sitting in a row on the edge of the wagon bed, their feet dangling. McGrother, the check lines in his hands, has his head turned back to speak to a man—a man whose name Old Jack cannot remember—who is standing on the step in front of the bank. The team and wagon are stopped in the middle of the road.

When Jack rides into the road and his horse's shod hooves strike the gravel, McGrother looks around and falls silent and looks away. His sons and the man on the bank step look away. It is in a strange silence, and as if unseen, that Jack moves now, and the ache of his anger is heavy in his chest. He can feel flaring at his temples the strokes of his heart. He stops the horse in front of McGrother, who is looking away. He leans and takes hold of McGrother's shoulder, and McGrother looks at him.

"I heard what you said, you God damned son of a bitch,"

With an abrupt shove he turns loose of McGrother's shoulder. He draws his foot from the stirrup and kicks McGrother's shins. He would like to see McGrother or his boys show some fight. He would be pleased to see them show some fight—any one or all three. He is drunk and ecstatic with his fury now. He does not care what happens. He does not care if he dies. Beside himself, he rides up and down the row of them, kicking their shins and cursing them in their faces. The two sons look away. McGrother struggles with his team to keep it from bolting. Around them the life of the town is stopped in its tracks and utterly silent. Spent finally, Jack turns and rides away.

He knew what he had risked. He knew even that he could not possibly know what retribution might rise upon the desperate terms of his wrath. What he remembers next could have come in retribution, but he was never sure.

The fire blooms on the frost of the back window like a winter dawn—to live in his mind for the rest of his life, though he looked at it only for an instant. The light touches everything in the room. He knows what it is. He does not look back at the window again. He is already up, pulling on his clothes and shoes. At the foot of the stairs, running now, he snatches his coat and hat off their nail and runs on across the frost-stiffened grass of the yard and the barn lot. The fire evidently started in the

hayloft, and everything above the loft floor is burning, the flames riding
high up against the sky, sparks from the burning hay swarming through
the skeleton of the roof and up the column of flame to swirl out at last
against the darkness. He can hear the cries and the violent stirrings of his
stock. He has twenty steers shut in a pen in the back of the barn, and he
runs there first, pulling open the doors and plunging into the heat and
the contained uproar of the fire that blasts and crackles over his head like
a windstorm in a forest. Shouting and beating with his hands, he drives
the cattle toward the door. They mass together. hesitating, held back as
if by an invisible fence arching across the opening. He shouts. He has
found a broken pitchfork handle now, and he lays it along their backs,
driving the ones in the rear hard up against the others. Suddenly one of
them leaps out the door and the others pour out after him, their hoof-
beats slurring off at a run into the dark pasture.

It is nearly too late, but he runs back through the driveway of the barn
and draws open one of the front doors. Taking his coat off as he goes, he
enters the stall of his saddle horse. With some effort, he gets hold of the
halter.

"Whoa! Whoa!"

He raises the coat. The horse whirls, throwing him hard against the
wall. Pain flashes in him. For a second he is on his knees, the horse dragging him, but he does not turn loose.

"Whoa!"

He eases the coat over the horse's head. The horse trembles now and
yields to his hand and is led out and released in the lot.

And that is all. There is no going in again. The driveway of the barn is
suddenly bright with fire. Three brood mares, a team of mules, and two
milk cows are still in there and they will burn. For what seems a long
time their cries fill the air around him.

Finally they are silent, and the sound of the fire seems to return. He
looks around. Three of his neighbors have come now. Together they fill
what buckets and barrels they can find and bring out a ladder so as to be
ready to protect the other buildings if need be. But there is no need. The
wind is out of the east, and the sparks are carried harmlessly away over
the fields. The four of them stand in a sort of formal row, facing the fire,

feeling the heat of it, saying little. So intent are they upon the fire that they are surprised after a while to see that the gray of dawn is already well into the sky, having slipped up behind them. The three neighbors leave to do their morning chores.

And now Jack stands there alone. He is nearly thoughtless, as if whatever there may be to think is still disassembled in the air around his head. The fire has nearly burned out. The barn is now only a heap of glowing ash that dulls to gray as the sky brightens. Ruth comes out, carrying the baby. Since she woke to hear Jack running out of the house she has watched from the kitchen window, weeping with horror and, yes, with pity for her husband. She has allowed herself to think that he may need her. And so she steps across the frozen grass in the dawn.

He stands there in front of her, his back to her, facing the ruin of the barn, whose little smokes drift up into the slowly brightening air. She sees how he stands there. Even now he keeps the easy straightness of a horseman that she has never seen bend in any weariness, that even in his old age will not bend. His hat tilted backward off his forehead, his coat unbuttoned, he stands with his feet a little apart, his hands hanging at his sides. He seems to her to stand as completely and finally where he is as a tree. His attitude reveals no surprise or shock or misery, and no pity for himself. It is the posture of a man who has already endured worse than he expected, and who knows that he can endure still worse. Seeing in that, perhaps, his mastery of a lesson that she has taught him, she slows her steps and then stops. She cannot go to him, nor for a while will she be able to return to the house.

A quietness has come over Jack. He knows that he is damaged. He knows that he is looking at what may be his ruin. He also knows that in a little while he will catch his horse and with a makeshift bridle ride bareback to town to see if he can borrow the money he will need to go ahead—to rebuild his barn, to buy new work stock and harness and all else that he will need to replace what has been destroyed. He already owes the bank, and so he will have to go to Ben—something he hoped never to do. But he is caught now. The boundaries of the old farm, which he so confidently thought to surpass, now contain him like walls. He who so short a time ago saw his work leading him to new land will now have to struggle for years to keep from losing the land he has. But he has come to the depths of a strange quietness in himself as he stands on the verge of his ruin, breathing the air.

He has heard Ruth come up behind him, but he cannot turn toward her. It will be some time yet before he will be able to bring himself to move at all. While the dawn comes, the two of them stand and do not move.

One of the posts of the barn is still standing, charred and smoking, the building burnt and fallen clean away from it, leaving it upright by itself, as plumb as the builders stood it. And now as Jack and Ruth stand there in one of the great turnings of their life, and as the sun rises and stains the white frost with its rosy light, a woodpecker comes up from the woods, its flight curving and dipping in the air, and clips itself to that blackened post. For an instant, just an instant, it is still and they see the vivid white and black of its wings, its head glowing red in the new light. And then it feels the heat. It cries once, casts off, and drops away down the slope of the ridge.

Five : Hunger

She is big. She feels big to herself, her breasts and belly swollen with life
that is hers, yet greater than hers. Quick in her now is the life that has
come like a pilgrim across the forgotten reaches of time, and is going on.
She feels it, the weight of it bearing insistently into her mind, thrusting
away from her. Though she is hurrying, she moves with a sort of deli-
cacy and deliberation such as one might use in maneuvering a heavily
loaded boat. Nearly eight months gone, she has felt the problem of balance slowly rising up into her consciousness until she has grown as attentive to it as a dancer who lifts his partner. Leaning back a little against the
weight of the child in her womb, she steps rapidly back and forth at her
work. The linoleum is smooth and cool under her bare feet. She remains
always a little conscious of her footing, of her body pivoting about its
shifted center.

She takes from the stove a pot of green beans, another of cabbage, a
dish of baked pears, a blackberry cobbler, and wraps each in newspaper
and sets it carefully into a cardboard box on the table. As she works her
face is preoccupied, deliberative, lighted as if from beneath the skin by a
serenity that lives upon her sense of being equal not just to what she is
doing but to whatever she has imagined she may have to do. It is a beautiful face, wreathed by dark, heavy hair, radiant from the touch of the
sun and her strong blood, the features clear. She is some years past the
simple prettiness of her girlhood. Her beauty no longer has its source

merely in her physical presence, though that is pleasing enough; it comes, rather, from some deep equanimity with which it has accepted the marks of an extraordinary knowledge of herself, her powers as a person and as a woman, her mortality. That understanding of mortality has been Hannah Coulter's great suffering, as now it is her peculiar gift; she has known and borne and accepted it upon the terms of her womanhood and her flesh. Before she became the wife of Nathan Coulter she had been for three and a half years the widow of Virgil Feltner, Mat's son, who, like Nathan's brother Tom, was killed in the second of the World Wars. And so she has learned by loss what it is she has. Her beauty now is the grace of her knowledge, a moving, level candor in her eyes. She has accepted the gift of mortality, loving a man's mortal love and her own given in return, her womb filled with a life that the earth will inherit.

She can hear Mattie squalling in the living room, but she is paying him no mind. She places the last of the dishes of food in the box and spreads a newspaper over them all and tucks it in around them. She straightens up, letting the trouble in the living room have her attention now, though she does not yet start out of the kitchen. On the wall over the sink is a shelf with Nathan's shaving things on it, and above the shelf a small mirror. Standing before the mirror, she hastily combs her hair, holding its silver clasp in her teeth, and then replaces the clasp and washes her hands at the sink. She goes to the back door where she left her shoes and puts them on. She looks around the kitchen again—everything that she is not to take with her is put away—and then she hastens into the living room to see what is the matter.

Mattie is sitting by himself in the middle of the floor, wailing in desolation, and his sister is on the couch, prim disgust on her face, pretending to read a book. Little Margaret is seven years old, blond, with something of the delicate prettiness of the girlhood pictures of her grandmother and namesake. She is pleased to be trusted to take care of Mattie, but because she is now fairly often capable of reasonable behavior she finds the unreasonableness of the little boy hard to put up with. At present he is offended because she made him be still while she put his shoes on him, and she is offended because he will not accept her efforts to comfort him.

Hannah bends down and swings the sad little boy up into her arms. "Well, goodness."

Mattie howls even louder to show the depth of his outrage.

"Mathew Burley Coulter, you *stop* that!"

He hushes, and sticks out his lower lip.

Hannah laughs. "Look at that face. Bring the washrag, hon," she says to the girl.

She carries Mattie over to the couch and sits down, holding him on her lap. It is getting on into the morning. The sunlight from the east window now makes only a narrow bar on the floor, drawn back nearly to the wall. Outside it will be hot. The men will be loading the wagons. "Margaret," she says.

Margaret comes with the washrag, and Hannah washes Mattie's face.

"You want to go to Granny's?"

The boy nods. His face changes. He is excited now. "I want to see Granddaddy."

"You can see him at dinner. And Papaw Coulter too."

"I want to see Papaw Coulter, and Uncle Burley."

"If Granny and Granddaddy are *my* daddy's parents," Margaret says, "then how can they be Mattie's grandparents?"

It is a question that she has been asking lately, in jealousy partly, but also in a sort of reaching toward the reality of her father's death. Earlier she used to ask directly to have his death explained to her; now she has grown sensitive to the pain in that and no longer mentions it. She asks instead about Mattie's relation to her grandparents, to symbolize by that the other question and to keep in touch with it. Hannah weaves again her life's complex bonds of love and kinship.

"For a long time once, when we needed them, Granny and Granddaddy took care of us, because we all loved each other. So I'm their daughter now because of that."

Margaret knows the story and likes it. Though she is little aware of the pain that was the making and the seal of that love, she feels its strength.

"And now Mattie and Granny and Granddaddy love each other too."

"That's right."

"And Daddy belongs to us all because he married you."

"Yep. And we all belong to him for the same reason. There!" Hannah puts Mattie down. "Now you're ready. You hold Margaret's hand."

She gets up, hurrying again, and goes back to the kitchen. The two children come along after her. Mattie is holding his sister's hand, minding. Things are going to suit him now.

"Go on out to the truck," Hannah tells them.

They go out across the back yard. She can hear them talking busily to each other. Though she cannot hear what they are saying, she pauses to listen. It is one of the good moments when both children are satisfied, and in their satisfaction she feels her own. She feels her house around her, quiet now, and around the house the quiet buildings and fields of the farm where today no one is at work. Now the children are out of earshot and there is no sound anywhere. She feels the silence reaching out like a live strand, binding her to her place. As always, when in such a silence she is most aware of herself, she is also most aware, even in his absence, of Nathan, and of what the two of them have dared to begin and to make out of war and death and loss, and what they hold together and continue now in the time of yet another war. She has not forgotten the prophecy she heard when she was a child, and which she has read many times since with recognition and without much doubt: "And ye shall hear of wars and rumors of wars. . . . For nation shall rise against nation, and kingdom against kingdom: and there shall be famines, and pestilences . . . woe unto them that are with child, and to them that give suck in those days!" She understands that woe. She knows that she does not know what will have to be suffered by the child drowsing in her womb. She mourns for the future, as the past has taught her. And yet there is a rejoicing in her, persistent and unbidden as the beating of her heart. There is a deep imperative in her flesh, not her mind's work but its strongest argument nevertheless, that tells her to step cheerful and quick. It alerts her to the welcoming hunger of the men who will soon be coming hot and weary from the field.

As she steps out into the day, the heat fits closely around her. She enters the brilliant ocean of it. It lies over the dry pastures with the yellow flowers of autumn blooming in them, and over the woods on the bluffs, and over the newly painted tin roofs that flash with aching brightness in it. After the cool night the air is without haze, the horizons deep and clear.

The kitchen that she has just stepped out of has a finished, composed look about it, suggesting that by the slow creation of use everything in it has found its place and become familiar. But out here, though the marks of use are everywhere, there is still the disorder of change. Nathan bought the place a little more than four years ago, shortly before he and Hannah married. At that time it was badly run down. Since then, while they have been living in it, they have labored at its renewal. The pastures have been cleaned up, the fences have been mended to forestall for a few years the expense of building them all again, four of the six rooms of the old house have been made livable, a water line has been laid from the well to the kitchen, and just before the tobacco cutting started Nathan and Burley painted the roof. But a lot either remains to be done or is in the process of being done. The newly painted roof makes it more noticeable than ever that the outside walls have not yet been painted. The back porch has been torn away from the house and not yet rebuilt; the old lumber, cleaned of nails, is piled nearby, waiting to be used again in the new porch. The bare ground where the porch stood is crossed by a makeshift walkway of old boards warping in the sun.

There are still plenty of eyesores; there is still plenty of work to be done, plenty to be desired. But the disorder is only in appearance—visible perhaps to a stranger's eye, but not to Hannah's, who knows the deeper order of intention and labor. As long as she and Nathan are here and able to work there will be order, if not in sight, then within reach. How long and carefully have they planned it, thought it out, talked it over? How many winter nights have they sat at the table, supper dishes put away, drawing out their plans on paper? So much, at least, of what lies ahead of them they have desired, foreseen, planned, pictured in their minds. Against all that they cannot foresee, against all dread, this is what excites her and hurries her on.

As soon as the present rush of work is over—when the tobacco is all in, here, at Mat's, at Burley's and Jarrat's, at Elton's, and the ground is sowed in grain to keep it over the winter—then they will build the new porch. It will be an enclosed porch, with lots of light for flowers, and space to wash and iron. She looks forward to the prettiness and the comfort of it. And she looks forward to its building. All the men will be here then, full of enthusiasm for the work. There will be a lot of talk and joking, much of it for her benefit. She will be called upon to consider and consult. The children will be full of the happiness of it. The work will have the pleasure and leisure that only fall work has, when the growing time is over and the crops are safe.

The milk cows are resting in the shade of the old white oak out by the feed barn. Two barred rock hens look irritably up at her from their dust holes under the snowball bush. She goes by with her load, looking around. No other breathing thing is in sight. The hot light weighs upon the earth, a sky-high hush. In the field, she knows, the men will be aware of that quiet, of the midday deep rest of things, of the shade-enclosed drowsing of beasts and, within that, of their own effort and weariness going on. They have been into it more than a week now, working long days, a lot ahead of them to do, and the tiredness and strain of it have begun to build up. She can tell it by the way Nathan turns and stirs at night, too wound up and anxious to lie still, even asleep.

Much of the night now she does not sleep, but she is not restless. She lies still, in a patience that makes her body one with the world, time passing, her time coming. It is as though she holds in herself, against darkness and even weariness, a bright cell of summer light. She grows full with the season, heavy with yield. It is a light that she recognizes as her own, though she is only its bearer. Now that she has come to know it, she knows she has never been without it. She has borne it to the men who have loved her; they have touched it in her, brought it to life. But only Nathan made her know it as her own.

When she looks back now, her time with Virgil seems remarkable for its innocence. They seem to her to have been almost children. Their love did not know what it risked. It did not know what it was going to cost. And now this second love has come, that *does* know, that has stood up in the world—as one who has been sick nearly to death and grown well again rises, wondering, in the mortal light, and stands and moves. A wondrous thing: she is a mortal woman, and she is not afraid.

Nathan rises and stands in her mind. She has always remembered Virgil, even while he lived, as turning toward her, seeking her, waiting for her to meet the asking of his gaze. In Nathan's absence she remembers him turning away, trusting her, depending on her, sure, not of her faith, but of herself, as she is sure. He will grin at her and turn away, going to the barn, going to work, leaving her to be what he knows she is. He makes no conditions. She is what she is. The day will be what it will, according to his intention and his strength, according to its weather and its chances. He grins—yes; all right—and leaves. This morning he had on an old shirt with the sleeves ripped off at the elbows. She thinks of his bare forearms, their smoothness, their piling and cording of muscle, their standing veins. The cell of light in her dilates and shines, crowding her heart.

She knees her load up against the side of the old truck to open the door, and then slides it in on the seat, not rattling a dish. The children are standing in the back.

"Here," she says. "Get up here next to the cab and sit down. Mattie, you hold Margaret's hand."

She goes around, yanks open the door on the driver's side, and gets in. She slams the door three times before it catches, jerks the choke out, stomps the starter. The truck is indomitably Nathan's, is apparently in some dumb fashion loyal to him; he drives it effortlessly. She can get nothing out of it without violence. She goes at it with a sort of utilitarian rage, shoves the choke halfway in, gives another punitive stomp to the starter. The engine catches, she guns it, backs through a cloud of blue smoke into the front yard, snatches the gearshift down into first. The old truck tumbles over the ledges of their lane to the road that follows the little stream known as Sand Ripple down to the river. She turns right, and they go up through the woods in the Sand Ripple hollow and out again into the open light of the upland. She comes to the blacktop at the schoolhouse hill beyond the edge of town and turns right again. She gets the old truck into high gear now and pours the juice to her.

They coast down past the barbershop at the foot of the hill and then, accelerating again, climb up past the stores, the post office, the bank, the hotel, the church, and turn, rattling, into Mat's driveway. When they stop the children are instantly scrambling over the tailgate.

Hannah gets out. "Listen! I want you both to mind now, and be good."

"We will," Margaret says.

"Mattie, did you hear me?"

"Yes."

Her warnings to Mattie always leave her with the impression that she has just spoken to a squirrel. She will take care of him when he needs it, which he will. Balancing her load, she follows them around the house to the kitchen door.

"Well, look who's come to see Granny," old Margaret says, opening her arms as Mattie runs to her to get hugged.

Little Margaret holds the screen door open for her mother, who steps in and sets the box down on the drain-board of the sink and stands waiting while Margaret finishes greeting the children—a big exchange of information. There is chicken frying on the stove, a baked ham, sugared and crisscrossed and spiked with cloves, lying ready to slice in the center of the table.

Now Little Margaret and Mattie go out to play in the back yard, and the two women set to work. Margaret gets the biscuits ready to go in the oven. Hannah peels and slices a platter of tomatoes. Before they are finished Mary Penn comes in, bringing her share of the meal: mashed potatoes, stewed tomatoes, creamed corn, a plate of dressed eggs. She is a lean, tall woman, brisk in her ways. When she speaks, it is always assumed that she is saying exactly what she means. She is wearing a plaid, short-sleeved blouse and denim pants, for when the meal is over and the dishes done she will go to the field to help the men—as Hannah would if she were not pregnant.

So many hands make quick work. Soon the table is set, the dishes of food made ready, the ham sliced, a bowl of cream whipped and sweetened for the cobbler. The two children are called in to eat and get done before the men come.

Margaret, who has been watching the window, says, "I see one of the loads coming. We can put the biscuits in." And then she says, "Uncle Jack ought to be here by now. I wonder where he is."

"I'll go get him," Hannah says.

The children want to go too but she tells them, "No. You finish eating," and goes out quickly before they can argue.

It is a moment of freedom she has now and she is glad of it. The work done behind her in the kitchen, she has the open day ahead of her for a few minutes, and then there will be the kitchen again, the hearty gathering in and feeding, the kitchen ritual of harvest. She feels good. She feels full of the goodness, the competency, of her body that can love a man and bear his children, that can raise and prepare food, keep the house, work in the field. She is living deep in her body now as she goes under the hot, bright sky into the town of Port William.

She sticks her head into Jasper Lathrop's store. "Uncle Jack here?"

"He was here early," Jasper says. He is leaning on his elbows, writing in a ledger that he has laid open on the counter. "He's been gone from here a couple of hours."

"I expect he's down to the barbershop," one of the loafers says above his baloney sandwich, not to her, to Jasper. "He was there while ago."

"Thanks."

She lets the screen door spring shut behind her and starts on down toward Jayber's shop. Now that she feels herself on Old Jack's trail she has him on her mind. She is aware of his isolation, his remoteness, now, from the daily life the rest of them are living. In the stillness of his old age he is beyond them, as though he looks back upon the world from a lofty island in the middle of a river. But she is aware of something else too. Over the last several months it has come to her that of all those near her Old Jack most carefully understands the fullness she has come to, and most exactly values it. From Mat and others she knows his story, or much of it, and knows that he recognizes her out of pain and loss. She is what he has failed. She is his consolation and his despair. How much of his vision of the world comes right in the figure of a woman fulfilled and satisfied, her man's welcomer, at home in the world! She is his Promised Land, that he may see but never hope to enter.

She steps out of the sun into the bouquet of the shop. That fragrant room is full of the deep stillness of midday. The conversation has broken up, the loafers having gone to dinner. Jayber is sitting in the barber chair, reading the paper. Old Jack is asleep.

Jayber grins sidelong at her from his perch. "Miz Totem, I believe."

"Hold your tongue."

"I have held little else. How's everybody?"

"All right. I've come for Uncle Jack."

Jayber motions toward the back of the room. Hannah nods.

"How is he?"

"He comes and goes. He's mostly gone, I think."

They have spoken quietly, but now Hannah lets the door slam and calls, "Dinner's ready, Uncle Jack."

Old Jack shakes his head and looks out. The room collects and rights itself in his gaze. "Ah Lordy!" he says. Hannah's voice has summoned him from a long time ago. And now he looks at her, smiling to find her there indeed.

He plants the cane and, holding to the crook of it with both hands, draws himself to his feet. Both Hannah and Jayber resist the impulse to help him. Though they have helped him in other ways, none of them has ever helped Old Jack to stand. It is a circumstance in which help would have to be too nakedly offered and accepted. It would be a violation. They leave him intact. He stands and approaches Hannah, removing his hat, offering his hand.

"Honey, I'm glad to see you."

"I'm glad to see you too," she says. She takes his hand, kisses his white-bristled cheek.

Old Jack's hand, which she continues to hold, is a fixed and final shape, bent and worn, curiously inert. The stiffened fingers no longer move with an idle life of their own. They lie still until he has a use for them and then they move by deliberate will, like rude tools. His hands remind Hannah of old gnarls of root such as she has found washed up on the rockbars of the river, still holding the shape of their place in the earth though that place is changed by their departure. She holds the old, clumsy hand in hers, gently, for its own sake. But for the sake of more than that, for she is thinking, "We will come to this, my Nathan."

"Come and eat dinner with us, Jayber," she says. "We'd be glad to have you."

"Oh, I guess I'd better stay here and mess up a little something for myself," Jayber says. "I'd be spoiled by good cooking." He says to Old Jack: "You'd better stay and have some dinner with me."

"I thank you, son." Old Jack says, signaling honor and gratitude to Jayber by a wave of his hand. "I know you can cook a meal of vittles as well as anybody, but the women, they'll be looking for me up at Mat's."

Jayber laughs silently, winking at Hannah, and reopens the newspaper. Hannah takes Old Jack's arm.

They walk slowly up the street toward Mat's, Hannah holding to the old man's arm as if to be helped, but in reality helping him. And yet she knows that, by taking that arm so graciously bent at her service, she *is* being helped. She is sturdily accompanied by his knowledge, in which she knows that she is whole. In his gaze she feels herself to be not just physically but historically a woman, one among generations, bearing into mystery the dark seed. She feels herself completed by that as she could not be completed by the desire of a younger man. As they walk, she tells him such news as there is: how they all are, where they are working, what they have got done, what they have left to do. From time to time she stops, as if to give all her attention to her story, to allow him a moment of rest. But she is glad to prolong the walk. She is moved by him, pleased to stand in his sight, whose final knowledge is womanly, who knows that all human labor passes into mystery, who has been faithful unto death to the life of his fields to no end that he will know in this world. As for Old Jack, he listens to the sound of her voice, strong and full of hope, knowing and near to joy, that pleases him and tells him what he wants to know. He nods and smiles, encouraging her to go on. Occasionally he praises her, in that tone of final judgment old age has given him. "You're a fine woman. You're all right," he says. And his tone implies: Believe it of yourself forever.

They are crossing Mat's yard now, and suddenly Old Jack can smell dinner. It is strong, and it stirs him. It changes his mind. He steps faster. He is leaving the world of his old age and entering a stronger, younger world. He is going into the very heart of that world where labor's hunger is fed with its increase. That is the order that he knows, and knows only and finally: that complexity of returns between work and hunger.

They turn the corner of the house into sight of the back porch, and there are all the men just come in. Two washpans and two kettles of hot water have been brought out and set down. Little Margaret stands nearby, holding a towel. Lightning and Mat's grandson, Andy Catlett, are washing at the edge of the porch, leaning over the pans. Mat is sitting in a willow rocking chair on the porch with Mattie on his lap. The others—Burley, Jarrat, Nathan, Elton—stand or squat in the yard beyond the porch, smoking, waiting their turns. Their shirts are wet with sweat. Their hands and the fronts of their clothes are dark with tobacco gum. They smell of sweat and tobacco and the earth of the field. In the stance of all of them there is relish of the stillness that comes after heavy labor. They have come to rest, and their stillness now, because of the long afternoon's work yet ahead of them, is more intense, more deeply felt, more carefully enjoyed, than that which will come at the day's end. Even Mat, who ordinarily would be carrying on some sort of play with Mattie, is sitting still, his hands at rest on the chair arms. Mattie is leaning against his shoulder, nearly asleep. Only Burley is talking, though he keeps otherwise as carefully still as the others. He is directing a mixture of banter and praise at Lightning's back. It is a bill of goods designed, as the rest of them well know, to keep Lightning on hand. Under the burden of such a stretch of hard work his customary bragging has given way to periods of sulkiness.

"Why, look at the *arm* on him," Burley is saying. "Look at the *muscle* the fellow's got. Damn, he can barely get his sleeve rolled up over it. No wonder I can't stay with him."

The others grin and wink. The fact is that, left to himself, Lightning is slow. But all week Burley has been working constantly at his heel, bragging on him, threatening to pass him, never quite doing it—and has succeeded in driving him almost up with Elton and Nathan, who are the best of them.

Lightning straightens from his washing and dries hands and face on the towel that Little Margaret holds out to him. He is doing his best to stay aloof from Burley's talk, but it gets to him, and he touches lovingly the muscle of his right arm.

"He put it on me this morning, Uncle Jack," Burley says, seeing the old man coming around the house. "I tried him, but I couldn't shake him."

"Go on and wash," he says to Jarrat. "I got to finish my smoke." He stands bent forward a little at the hips, hand on the small of his back. He seems to be hurting a little. He probably is, but he is playing on it too, parodying an aged and a beaten man. He looks afar, soliloquizing about his defeat. "Nawsir! Couldn't handle him! Too few biscuits and too many years have done made the difference."

"Ay Lord, he's a good one!" Old Jack says, seeing the point. He knows where that Lightning would be if somebody was not crowding him all the time. Somewhere asleep. But he shakes his head in approbation of Burley's praise. "He's got the right look about him."

"You're right, old scout," Burley says. "He's the pride of Landing Branch, and no doubt about it. But I believe I smell a biscuit in the wind, and maybe a ham, and that may make a difference this afternoon. When I go back out there I aim to be properly fed. Oh, I may not get ahead of him, but I'll be where he can hear me coming. Ham and biscuits!" he says. And he sings:

> How many biscuits can you eat?
> Forty-nine and a ham of meat
> This mornin'.

Lightning is at work now with a comb, putting the finishing touches to his wave and ducktail, a sculpture not destined to survive the next motion of his head. There is an arrogance in his eye and jaw and the line of his mouth, based not upon any excellence of his own but upon his contempt for excellence: if he is not the best man in the field, then he is nevertheless equal to the best man by the perfection of his scorn, for the best man and for the possibility that is incarnate in him. Old Jack studies Lightning's face—he recognizes it; he has known other men who have worn it, too many—and then he grunts, *"Hunh!"* and looks away.

Jarrat and Elton finish washing and Burley and Nathan take their places. Hannah picks up Mattie, who has fallen asleep in Mat's lap, and takes him in to his napping place on the parlor floor. Little Margaret has wandered off to play.

Now Mat gets up and he and Old Jack wash. When they have finished with the towel, Mat hangs it on the back of the rocking chair.

"Let's go eat it," he says. He holds open the kitchen door and they file in past him, Old Jack first and the others following. There is a general exchange of greetings between the men and the three women.

Old Jack takes his place at the head of the table. "Sit down, boys," he says, and they pull out their chairs and sit down. Mat is at the foot of the table. At the sides, to Old Jack's right, are Elton and Lightning and Andy and, to his left, Burley and Nathan and Jarrat. They pass the various loaded platters and bowls, filling their plates.

They fall silent now, eating with the concentration of hunger. The women keep the dishes moving around the table as necessary and keep the glasses filled with iced tea.

"Lay it away, boys," Old Jack says. "It's fine and there's plenty of it."

Following his lead, the others praise the food, the ones whose wives have cooked being careful to praise the cooking of the other women.

In the presence of that hunger and that eager filling, Old Jack eats well himself. But his thoughts go to the other men, and he watches them. He watches the older ones—Mat and Jarrat and Burley—sensing their weariness and their will to endure, troubling about them and admiring them. He watches the five proven men, whom he loves with the satisfaction of thorough knowledge and long trust, praising and blessing them in his mind. He watches them with pleasure so keen it is almost pain.

And he watches the boy, Andy, whom he loves out of kinship and because he is not afraid of work and because of his good, promising mind, but with uneasiness also because he has so little meat on his bones and has a lot to go through, a lot to make up his mind about.

And he watches Lightning, whom he does not love. That one, he thinks, will be hard put to be worth what he will eat. For he is one who believes in a way out. As long as he has two choices, or thinks he has, he will never do his best or think of the possibility of the best.

Old Jack shakes his head. "See that that Andy gets plenty to eat," he tells Mat.

"Don't you worry. I'm going to take care of this boy," Mat says. And he gives Andy a squeeze and a pat on the shoulder.

"We going to miss old Andy when he's gone," Burley says.

The edge is off their hunger now, and they give attention to Andy, for whom this is the summer's last workday. Tomorrow he will be leaving to begin his first year of college.

"We'll be looking around here for the old boy," Burley says, "and he'll done be gone. They'll say, 'Where's the old long boy that could load the wagon so good? Where's that one that used to house the top tiers?' And we'll say, 'Old Andy ain't here no more. He's up there to the university, studying his books.'"

"Studying the girls," Nathan says, grinning and winking at Hannah.

"He'll be all right with the girls if he wants to be," Hannah says. "I'm a better judge of that than you."

"You do all right with Kirby, don't you, Andy, hon?" Mary Penn says.

"Yeah, if old Kirby's going to have any say-so, he *better* keep his mind on his books while he's up there," Burley says. "He don't, she'll kick over the beehive, I expect."

"You keep your mind on your books anyhow, Andy," Jarrat says, looking gravely across the table at the boy, his gaze ponderous and straight under thick brows. "Mind your books, and amount to something."

"Andy," Elton says, "you'll get full of book learning and fine ways up there, and you won't have any more time for us here at all."

Andy, who has been grinning at this commentary on his departure, now flushes with embarrassment. "Yes I will," he says, though he knows the inadequacy of such an avowal. The faith that Elton has called for, though he spoke in jest, will have to be proved.

They all know it. Andy has not yet chosen among his choices.

And then Mat says, "Well, he's learned some things here with us that he couldn't have learned in a school. A lot of his teachers there won't know them. And if he's the boy I think he is, he won't forget them."

"Yessir!" Old Jack says. "By God, that's right!"

Now all the plates are empty. The women gather them and stack them by the sink. They replace them with dishes of blackberry cobbler, still warm from the oven, covered with cold whipped cream.

"You all can thank Andy for this," Hannah says. "I made it for him because it's his favorite."

"*Thank* him!" Nathan says. "I'm mad as hell about it. When are you going to fix me something because it's *my* favorite?"

Hannah grins. "Your time is coming," she says, "*junior.*"

The others laugh. The iced tea glasses are filled again. They take their time over the cobbler, talking idly now of the past, of other crops.

The afternoon's work is near them, not to be put off much longer. Old Jack can feel it around him in the air, that dread of the heat and heaviness of the afternoon that even the strongest and the best man will suffer. But not for him any more the going back to the field. No more for him the breaking sweat under the sun's blaze, the delight of skill and strength, and the pride.

He returns to himself as he was when he was a breaker of horses. For that was one of his economies and one of his earnings after the disaster of the barn. The fire had cleaned him of work stock except for one gray mare mule, an excellent plow mule by the name of Queen that he had lent the summer before to Ben Feltner. Needing then to save every possible penny, he agreed to take a pair of young mules from Ben and break them in return for the use of them through the crop year. And he did. He had always broken his own work and saddle stock, and so the art of it was known to him. Working the young mules at first separately, hitched with Queen, and then together, he made a team of them, and carried on his work in the process.

Soon the word got around, and he was given other stock to break—horses and mules of all kinds, occasionally a saddle horse, but he had little time to spare for that, and mostly he stuck to work stock. It was tricky, dangerous work for a man to do alone. But he was good at it. He was skillful. He knew what was possible. He knew, in any circumstance, what was apt to happen.

He liked it. The danger of it was giving him back the feel of his life—as Ruth and his work, blighted by debt, no longer could. Working the young teams, always on the lookout against tooth and hoof, alert for the blowing leaf or flying bird that would start them running, using by turns skill and main strength, he lived on the narrow line between life and death, in deeper touch than he had been in ten years with the intricacy of power and skill that made his manhood.

There was something fine about it. Something rare. To take a pair of young horses, after he had worked them sufficiently with the gray mule, and hitch them together for the first time as a team: harness them, stand them side by side along the wagon tongue to snap the check lines to their bits, talking to them to keep them settled and quiet (it is all up in the air now, like a young bird learning to fly, moving tensely from one point of assurance to another), then fasten the breast chains (talk easy, be quiet and quick), then the traces (here's where you watch their feet; "Whoa, boy"), and take the reins in one hand and ease up into the wagon. He is standing in the wagon now, with the reins in his hands. He speaks to them—"Come up"—bringing it all together. Ah!

Dessert is finished. They have smoked. There comes a long moment of suspension between the conclusion of the meal and the return to work. An ancient anguish builds among them now, especially among the older ones, who know best that it is inescapable. Old Jack can feel it. Here they are, out of the sun, at rest, drinking for the pleasure of it the trickles of water melted from the ice in their glasses. And outside the sun is blazing, not a breath of wind stirs, the loads wait. They are again at the gate of Eden, looking out. Again they must resume their journey, the long return of dust to dust.

And then Mat pushes his chair back. "Boys," he says quietly, "let's go, let's hit it. Andy, you fill the water jugs." And he gets up.

It was Mat's place to say those words, and Old Jack has heard them with relief and joy. Mat is sixty-eight years old, past the workdays of a lot of men in these times, his hair white. And yet there he stands, sore and tired, able and ready, telling them, "We ain't getting it done setting here, boys." Old Jack looks up at Mat, his sister's son. The window flares in his gaze, a wall of light.

The others pick up their hats and caps from the floor and scrape their chairs back and get up, Burley and Jarrat, like Mat, standing bent at the hips; every time they stop and start again, there is the stiffness to be worked out. They put on their hats, joking at each other—"Going to be just a leetle warm up under that barn roof, Andy boy"—and follow Mat out the door. In no time the sound of their footsteps has died away and the silence is large in the room. The women clear the table of bowls and spoons and glasses, set places for themselves, and sit down to eat. It is a quietness and a leisure that they have coveted while they prepared the meal and served it and they take their time with it. Margaret is speaking of Andy's impending departure with a simplicity that is characteristic of her.

"I don't *want* him to go," she says, "but I know it's right. The Lord gave him a good mind. That's what I think about."

Mary Penn laughs. "Well, maybe he'll learn to use it for something. Lord, he's a dreamy one, that kid. Elton says he'd be a fine hand if he could just keep his mind on what he's doing."

"He's a good old boy, though," Hannah says. Andy confides in her. She knows something of where his mind goes when it leaves his work.

"He *is* a good boy," Margaret says. "He's never worn out a hat in his life for forgetting where he leaves them, but he's a good boy. Of course, as his grandaddy says, there's a lot he'll have to get past. He'll have to try out some things."

"Wouldn't you like to have a glimpse of him trying out that city life," Mary Penn says, "and him not know you were looking?"

"No," Margaret says. "I don't think I would."

Old Jack seems to doze, and they go on as if he is not there. But he is not asleep. He is deeply and quietly awake in the climate of women, the talk and the domestic warmth of women at ease among themselves, and he is basking in it. He has been a long time coming to it, this temperate zone, but here he is at last. It is a goodness not of his making, he knows. What he feels here, this ease of women, has been made by them and their men in darknesses strange to him. Though he has come close enough to it in his time to recognize it, he has made no such thing. But he is an old man, and he has not come here by contrivance or deceit; say rather that this warm surrounding has come to him unasked, a blessing, and he will stay in it as long as he can. He stays until their meal is finished, until the drawers are shut and the cabinets closed, until Mary Penn goes to join the men at work, until Mattie wakes from his nap and Hannah prepares to start home.

He gets up then and thanks Margaret and Hannah, patting their shoulders so as to touch them with the direct gravity of his praise, and goes out. He starts back down into town, taking his time. The passivity of his old age is beginning to afflict him now, the sense of having nothing to do, no intention; his afternoon will fill itself with what he will *let* happen, not what he will *make* happen.

The town is filled with light. The shadows of the trees along the street have begun to stretch eastward, but not much. Every surface glints with a hard, piercing brightness. The steeple of the church thrusts its point into a sky that swells and aches with light. His eyes seek the shadows to rest in. An old black-and-tan coonhound is asleep on the maple-shaded sidewalk in front of Jasper Lathrop's house. No other man or beast is in sight. A gust of sparrows rounds the weeping willow in Mamie Spanker's yard and flies over the roof of the hotel.

He goes by the church and its crony, the bank. Just below the bank he stops, for he has heard from far back the sound of an empty wagon drawn swiftly over a rough road. And now he feels shuddering in his body the jolt and chatter of the ironshod wheels over the rocks. He is angry at Ruth and he has wasted half the day. He is headed home as fast as the wagon will travel over that road and hold together.

The cause of his anger is trivial enough perhaps. Or the immediate cause is. When he came in to dinner Ruth said, "Jack, I have baking to do, and I'm nearly out of flour."

It was a dangerous admission and she knew it. Here it was only Wednesday and he had been to the store at the landing on Saturday. He was hurrying to get his crops plowed before laying them by.

"I'm sorry," she said, bridling at the exasperation in his eyes. "I didn't realize the barrel was getting so low."

"By God, I'm sorry too," he said. "That's a long drive down there and back for nothing."

"For nothing! I assume you want to eat."

"And I assume, damn it to hell, that you want a living made for you. If I farmed the way you run this kitchen we'd be short more than a barrel of flour."

"That is *not* true."

He knew the truth. She was right, and it made him madder than ever.

"And *don't* you speak to me in that language."

"I'll speak as I God damn please."

They fought it out among those trivial issues that later, as always, would shame them both. And yet the quarrel had the same real subject as all their quarrels: the failure of each of them to be what the other desired. The subject was loneliness and sorrow. Between them now no grievance was too trivial to reach directly into that anguish that was costing them their hopes.

He ended it by leaving the house without eating. He hitched a team to the wagon and set out for the landing. Except for what she most desired, he could deny her nothing. Both of them knew that. But it was also his way of punishing himself for his failure to win her. In the desperate symmetry of their tragedy, what was true of him was true of her: she could deny him nothing, except what he most desired.

He drove the four miles in to Port William and then the mile down from Port William to the landing only to find that they were out of flour;

they were expecting a boat but it had not come. The trip was for nothing, as he had said. His anger assumed the dark gladness of vindication. By then it was starting to rain, and he had to tie the team and take shelter in the store. There was an hour's hard downpour. That put an end to plowing for a while. Unless the worst of the storm had somehow missed his place, he knew that his crops and his fields too had been damaged. He dreaded what he would see when he got home.

The necessity of conversation while he waited in the store made an abeyance of his mood. But once he was by himself again on the road home, his anger, now compounded by the uselessness of the trip and anxiety about the damages of the storm, returned to him. Now on the levels and the downgrades he touched the horses with his whip, urging them into a trot. The road ditches were flowing full of muddy water. The foliage along the embankments bent low with the weight of the beaded rain. Several times he had to get down and drag a fallen branch out of the road.

The day had turned altogether wrong. It had opened that cleft, that desert place in his life, between him and Ruth, field and house, desire and realization. As always when new failure opened it to him, that vacancy was filling with the aimless demon of his fury.

He passed back through the town and turned onto the Birds Branch Road. The road followed the ridges for a mile or so and then reached the lip of the creek valley. From there he could see the muddy currents of the creek risen over the ford. He could not yet tell how high the water was, but if he could not cross he knew he would have a long wait. He would have to sit and wait while gravity at its leisure drew the runoff down from the ridges. While he looked he allowed the team to stop. Again he touched them with his whip, sending them into the descent.

Now he stands with his knees flexed against the jolt of the wagon, enclosed and suspended in the pounding and clattering of the wheels. He is halfway across the bottom and he can see the creek again. It is higher than it looked from above. Over the shoal of the ford the standing waves look at first like a flock of brown hens feeding, and then he sees a tree trunk tossed down among them. But he does not slow the team. As though watching himself from far off, with a strange, calm judgment of foreknowledge, he knows what he is going to do. He plunges, rattling, into the no man's land of his despair. In opposition to darkness he has shut his eyes and called up a darkness of his own. He is standing in the attitude of a man ready to leap. In his throat there is a swelling as of laughter.

For an instant, where the road makes its final brief downturn above the water, the horses' hind hooves brake and skid over the rocks. But he shouts and lays on the whip, and they yield to him and go on. He takes them tightly in hand now as they throw their heads up and go into the water, the current sucking and pouring loudly around them. They are a young team of sorrels—another that he has taken to break—big and strong, work hardened, thoroughly responsive to him, and for a time as he stands leaning there above them it seems to him that they will make it. But the water is already over his shoes in the wagon bed. The brown current piles and beats against the sideboard on the upstream side, beginning to slosh in. Beneath him now he can feel the wheels edging downstream as they turn. And then, with a motion that is serene, almost stately, in the midst of the turbulence and striving, the wagon floats free.

He calls on the horses, his voice calm and quieting, as if he had foreseen it all and is not surprised, as if he has been through this before and knows what to do. He has moved instinctively to the upstream side of the wagon to hold it down and keep it from rolling in the current. But now the wagon is swinging downstream, turning the horses and dragging them backwards. They are losing their purchase on the ground. He sees it all come loose and turn in the water. It is like falling.

Again he knows what to do. He is working now as if the job is familiar to him and he follows a plan. He springs from the headboard of the wagon onto the back of his lead horse. He gets out his knife and cuts reins and checkreins. And now—he does not know what happened; maybe something snagged the wagon and held it momentarily—he and horses and all are under water. He clings to the horse's back and to the knife. They come up choking in the pool below the ford. Though the current remains strong there is no turbulence here, and he finishes his work, cutting the top hame strings and backbands to free the horses of the harness and wagon. As the horses struggle loose and begin to swim, he leans out and catches the rein of the off horse's bridle.

They go into the next rapid, Jack having time only to slip his arm through the collar of the horse he is riding and turn the off horse's rein once around his hand. This time he loses his seat on the horse's back, but he holds to collar and rein and is dragged through, all three of them going under again in the suck at the foot of the plunge. In the next stretch of quiet water he gets astride the lead horse again. They reach the edge of the stream, climb the bank, and stop at last in a little grove of sycamores. He slides to the ground. And now the energy of his fury goes. His knees will scarcely support him. He grasps the collars of the two horses and holds on. He hangs between them, dripping and trembling. It will be some time before he can stand alone.

Six : Rose

Present vision returns to him, re-enters his head and looks out like a woodpecker in an old tree. Maple foliage rears above him like a breaking wave. Beyond its shade the light beats and glances upon the town as it floats, slowly rising and sinking, in the light. For a moment desire and grief, the old famine of his loins, live in his flesh again. And then he feels the coolness of the shade. Though the beginning seems to him strangely disturbing, a derangement of permanent order, as though a tree should walk, he moves.

In front of Burgess's store there is a bench that he knows he can have to himself, for at this time of day it is in the sun. He goes there. He needs the sun. Though his plunge into the flooded stream, his dark and airless struggle in the waves, is behind him once again, this time he has kept the chill of it. He is a man wrapped in shade.

He reaches the bench and sits down. He becomes deeply still again under the pouring light. The warmth of it touches his skin and reaches into his flesh. Eyes shut, head tilted back, hands at rest upon his cane's crook, he sinks immeasurably down and down into a well of light as warm and red as blood. He has met the sun at its entrance to the earth, where it is blooded and then darkened. It burns away the shadow and ash of the flesh of his old age, and he lives again, light and strong, in his mind. And now, as if out of an old history living in his hands, returns to him the presence and the touch of her who loved him as he was.

Rose McInnis. Rose. She had become, soon after her twentieth birthday, the wife of an old doctor of the community, Clay McInnis. Why she should have consented to such a marriage Jack never heard, and she never said. The town, as usual, was willing to supply any motive that was not announced. She had married him, had seduced him into marriage, the town declared, in order to inherit his farm and other worldly goods, for which it was thought that he would soon have no further use. He lived thirteen more years—to Rose's deep consternation, the town supposed, though it did not know, for Rose and her old doctor passed those years quietly, mainly within the bounds of the tiny farm, with its brick cottage and log barn, on the town's edge. The doctor's practice had been largely taken up by a younger man, and only a few of the old patients remained faithful and came to the cottage to be cured, or if not cured then at least soundly lectured, by old McInnis whose indignation against the weaknesses of the flesh became stronger as his own flesh weakened. Rose surrounded the little house with flowers and kept a garden, a flock of hens, and a cow. She knew the town's judgment of her, but though the decent, comfortable life she made for her old husband deserved a better one, she signified no wish to have it changed. She kept to herself, asked for nothing, and on her infrequent trips to the store to make purchases or to market eggs and cream, there would be a tightness in the corners of her mouth, a certain tilt to her head, suggesting that she had made a judgment of her own.

The death of the old doctor did not change her life—a fact that the town found more enduringly worthy of notice and comment than any change it might have made. If she had quickly remarried, or sold everything and moved away, the town would have noted with pleasure the fulfillment of its expectations and turned to other matters. But the old doctor made his silent trip to the graveyard and things went on as before. The farmer who had grown the crops on the little place went on growing them. When her cow was fresh and her hens were laying, Rose appeared at regular intervals, walking through town with a basket of eggs and a bucket of cream. The little house looked the same as ever: in winter lonely and small beneath the halted black fountain of its old elm; in summer half buried in flowers, veiled in bee hum and bird song. Port William knew no other place like it.

And now it is gone: the cottage gutted by fire and the bricks carried away, the log barn rotted into the ground, the other buildings gone by fire or wind or rot, the elm and the fruit trees gone. All gone, and the ground grown over with grass. Perhaps he alone remembers it. It stands clear in his mind, light and fragrance around it.

To the few who were led by business or good fortune through the gate in the picket fence in the summertime, the cottage's surroundings seemed to recall ancient happy memories or dreams. One walked between two huge mock orange bushes inside the gate and emerged deep in flowers. A walk of square-hewn limestone slabs led to the doorstep and turned to go around the side of the house under the branches of apple trees. In the back, in the angle between the bedroom and the porch of the kitchen ell, there was a brick pavement with a well in its center. In the heat of the day this area, like the house itself, was shaded by the great elm that stood on the other side of the kitchen. Beyond, to the left, there was a fenced poultry yard with a row of plum and cherry trees down the middle, and to the right, divided from the poultry yard by a hedge of lilac bushes, a vegetable garden. The whitewashed outbuildings gleamed in the sun. The order and abundance of the place seemed the emanation of a deeply indwelling artistry. Whatever this woman touched flowered and bore. A peculiar thing was that those infrequent ones who came there, though they praised flower and vegetable and fruit, never asked her how she grew them. It was as though they suspected, in the unfaltering dark eyes that seemed to judge their praise, the knowledge of some mystery that they could not choose to know. Many who came there went away thinking, "I would like to live in such a place." And not a few who came there thought, "Once, long ago, I must have lived in such a place."

Jack had known her distantly from the time of her marriage to the doctor. That is, when he saw her he knew who she was. Beyond that he accepted the town's verdict that she was "odd." And then, in the fall, a year or two before the doctor's death, he cut his leg severely with a corn knife. Will Wells was still with him then. They had put in a long day, cutting the standing corn and bundling it into shocks. It was getting on toward dark. Jack, faltering in the work's rhythm, perhaps because of the cold, made a misstep and slashed his left leg across the calf, just below the knee. For some time he tried to ignore it and go on—the moon was full and early risen, and they had thought to keep on into the evening. But the wound would not stop bleeding. They could hear the blood squelching in his boot. Such bindings as they could contrive all failed to stanch it. Finally Will gave into the moonlight the laugh he laughed when he sensed the futility of a thing.

"Mr. Jack, you best go get that seen to."

"I reckon I had," Jack said. And leaving Will to finish the shock they had started and then do up the chores, he went to the barn for his horse and rode to Dr. McInnis's.

He hitched his horse at the fence and went to the door and knocked. Footsteps—not the doctor's—approached through the house. The door opened on the silhouette of a woman poised against the glow of an oil lamp on the table in the room behind her.

"Yes?"

"I want to see the doctor."

"He's been out. He's eating supper. What's the matter?"

"I cut my leg." He points.

And then this woman, instead of doing any of the several things that he would have expected—instead of calling the doctor, or inviting him to come in, or telling him to wait—this woman steps out of her own light and bends down and opens the cut in his pantleg and looks briefly, knowingly, at his wound. Her hands go to him unhesitatingly, without apology.

"I'd say you whacked it a good one. You'd better come on in."

He follows her into the sitting room, watching her with interest now, and pleasure too, though she remains a shadow between him and the light.

"Sit down." She points to a straight-backed chair near the hearth where a log fire is burning. "I'll get the doctor."

After a minute or so she follows the doctor into the room. The doctor is still chewing his last bite of supper. He has his satchel in his hand. Rose is carrying another lighted lamp, which she sets on the mantlepiece. By its light for the first time he looks at her face—her good, lean, dark face; its impulsive flashings of teeth and eyes—and finds her looking back at him, grinning.

"I guess you had to miss a lot else to hit that, didn't you?"

He grins back. "I did for a fact."

The old doctor pulls up a chair to face Jack's and sits down. "Let's see it." No greeting, no recognition, as usual. He has come to uncompromising terms with his lot. The sick and the maimed come to him, and he does what is necessary, or he does what is possible, or he does what he knows how to do. That the various complaints and wounds are borne by particular creatures is merely incidental, as is, by now, the creatures' ability to pay.

Rose brings a pan of hot water and some clean rags, and the doctor, who has greatly lengthened the cut in Jack's pantleg with his knife, begins to wash the wound. Rose gives Jack a table glass half full of whisky. He takes a sip.

"Drink it," she says, and he does.

"Here," the doctor says without looking up, and Rose stoops to help him. He instructs her with monosyllables and grunts as he cleans the cut and goes to work with his suture. He sews the gaping flesh together, as brusquely unconcerned as if he were sewing up a hole in a sack, but with marvelous accuracy and speed for such shaking old hands. The stabs of the needle transform Jack's body into a new substance dilating with pain. He holds tightly to the chair seat and keeps still, because of the whisky or the pain or both filling with anger. When the stitching is over at last, he lets it out: "That's my *leg,* old man!"

At that Rose, who is tearing rags to make a bandage, looks straight into his eyes and laughs. And then, the whisky loosening him, he laughs. "Oh my God," he says, "that was one of 'em!"

The doctor binds the wound and knots the ties of the bandage. And only then, holding the bound leg in both hands as though testing or savoring the completion of yet another job, does he look at Jack's face.

"Now Goddamn it, son, listen to me. Stay off of that leg for a week."

Jack gets up and pays him and leaves, his split pant-leg flapping. He rides home, light with whisky and pain, the country all around him astir with the cold wind, the full moon at his back.

He did not stay off the leg for a week. He went back to work the next morning, limping. The leg healed as he insisted it would. And he bore Rose McInnis in his mind.

How things were for a while after that he does not remember. He remembers the old doctor's death, and the speculative and inquisitive conversation that the town carried on afterwards about Rose and her "oddness." And then he began to meet her eyes again. In one or another of the stores or along the road as he was riding by, he would look up and she would be looking at him. And it was the other way around, too: sometimes when she looked up he would be looking at her. How this should have been or how it came about he does not quite know. Were they slowly approaching each other by some deep-held intention? Or were they drawing together unintentionally, as two trees will lean toward each other and finally touch, reaching toward the same opening? Only that there was great need there is no doubt. That there was great desire, that she bore toward him the hunger for which he hungered, there is no doubt.

Did not the intention reside in the fact? Perhaps it was as simple as that. How, with her eyes' swift clarities upon him, could he have thought what his intention *had* been? He was quiet enough within himself now to offer and respond. Since his escape from the flooded stream he had been changed. He had ceased to resist his old failures. He no longer asked from his marriage what he knew was not in it. Now he contained his loneliness in himself and stood free.

And so when he felt himself sought for and found by Rose's eyes, he was entirely present before her. And she stood entirely before him. She stands before him now, as then, a woman with the stature of a young tree, with a good straight look in her eyes, inviting him to desire her and to think well of himself. He holds himself deep in his mind, in his competent flesh of those old days, in her presence. Her memory surrounds him, a fragrance or an ecstasy that he will not turn from, though he knows what it will cost him. He cannot turn away from her now. Here where she has not walked or stood or turned to look for fifty years, she holds him as before.

They had not had occasion to speak since the night of his visit to the doctor. A complex understanding had grown between them before they ever spoke. They met always in public, always at a distance. The silent looks that passed between them held them at once together and apart. They waited, he waited, perhaps because of a sense of what a powerful thing, between them, speech would finally be. Their first words, he knew, would change them and change their world.

And then one fine morning in the spring—there had been rain; the ground was too wet to work; he was in town to buy seed—he felt an old grace upon him. This time, when he passed the cottage and saw Rose in the yard, he did not ride by, but rode up to the fence and stopped. She came toward him, stepping slowly along the stones of the walk and into the gate. She looked up at him, smiling, knowing—she had known, surely, for a long time—what he would say.

"I'm going to come to see you tonight," he said.

The words made a sudden clarity between them, and a new silence. For some time they waited again, aware of their breathing. And then, not smiling, with a look that held to no condition or equivocation, that left them no way out, she said: "I'll look for you."

Her look and her words moved him so that he shuddered. The horse felt it and stirred restlessly beneath him. He rode on.

And darkfall brought him back, true to his word. He worked until sundown, and then did his chores and ate supper and cleaned up. He went back to the barn and saddled his horse. When he rode past the house Ruth already had a lamp burning in the sitting room. He often rode out at night to carry on the business connected with his work or his debts, and no explanation was required of him. He passed by the lighted house in the dark, a powerful direction rooted in his mind.

When he approached the end of the Birds Branch Road he met a buggy returning from town. When it was out of sight he stopped his horse and for a moment waited. The night was clear, the moon past a quarter full. His brief pause was not hesitation, but a summoning of himself before the time, a deliberate gathering of himself: "Yes, this is the way I am going to go now." And again he shuddered, a swift dilation of the flesh. He spoke to the horse and they went on. He went through a gate, crossed the fields well back of town, and turned into a wooded draw that he knew would bring him up behind the cottage garden.

Now he comes up through the woods, among the great looming trunks of the old trees. Underfoot the last year's leaves are wet; walking over them, the horse's hooves are nearly silent. He can hear, receding behind him, the preoccupied voice of the little stream in the bottom of the draw. He can hear the voices of frogs and whippoorwills, those also at a distance. The far-off sounds make the quiet where he is all the greater and deeper. In the little light that filters down through the branches, he can see white flowers faintly glowing on the floor of the woods, and in that light the trees are presences more felt than seen.

He hitches his horse to a sapling at the edge of the woods, and from there goes on foot out again into the open. He makes no noise at all. He can hear the sound of his breath. He goes by the barn and through a little gate into the back of the garden, careful not to make a sound—not that it matters, but the silence is around him now like a law. The broken ground of the garden is dark on his left. He follows a grassy walk along the edge of it. The fragrance of the lilacs has come over him now, and from the top of the old elm he can hear the triple repetitions of the song of a mockingbird. He goes on past the corner of the poultry yard, treading flagstones under the heavy shadow of the elm. Darkness and silence reach far behind and ahead of him. It is as if he is falling, a sweetness of abandon in him that he has not felt for years. An old music that he remembers well sounds again ahead of him in the distance. A thoughtless dark fragrance fills his mind. His hands are light at his sides. And then behind him the poultry yard gate shuts with a light knock, and he stops and turns. The quiet completes itself again. And then Rose's voice asks: "Who is it?"

There is a flash in his nerves then that he will remember half a century. For a moment, while the countryside seems to tilt underfoot and then slowly come level again, he does not answer. And then he says: "Jack Beechum."

In the shadow of the elm he cannot see her until she materializes in his reach, the light of her face borne upon shadow. He feels her hand light upon his face.

"I know you, Jack Beechum," she says.

She knew him as he was, and loved him. He was naked before her and was not ashamed. Into the good darkness that she offered him he went again and again. Something of his old gladness returned to him. He worked through the long days eager for the night to fall.

The town's ever-vigilant curiosity, which saw in the dark, found them out. And he did not care. The talk went around under cover of righteousness. Need was the cause of it. The little groups that the talk stirred in the stores and the kitchens and the street were like people lighting torches at a fire. It was as if Jack and Rose, like other lovers before and after them, had been elected to stir from the ashes of pretense and fear the light of a vital flame. While it condemned them the town needed them and praised them in the darkness of its heart. The town talked and looked askance, and waited eagerly for more news out of that dark and fragrant garden from which it felt itself in exile. And so this coupling went into the town's mind, to belong to its history and its hope, even against its will. Even as the knowledge of it fades, it remains, an inflection of the heart, troubling and consoling the night watches of lonely husbands and wives like a phrase from a forgotten song.

Jack knew all that, and he did not care. He knew that Ruth knew, or would sooner or later know, and he did not care. He would not let himself care. He knew that he might come to care, that he might, later, *have* to care. But he would not care yet. For the flame that the town desired and envied and secretly praised he had now turned openly toward. He knew that Rose had restored his life, that she had reached with her honest, eager hands and touched and revived that energy, that wild joy in him, that Ruth had all but destroyed with her fastidiousness and her shame.

He would care for Rose. He would care for the workings of the dark and the ground that she had newly alerted him to. He would care for the cottage and its garden and the great elm that stood like a guardian over it. He would care for the night's coming, and for the light that his desire cast around him, and for his arrival at the door, and for their talk and laughter falling to silence. And for nothing beyond the reach and touch of Rose would he care now, for there was a joy in him that overrode all outside itself, she had so imparadised his mind. She so received and welcomed him, and made him such delight, that it seemed to him his very life struggled and broke free and passed into her, and he lay in the dark beside her in a strange sleep, empty of strength and thought as a dead man. He went away from her newborn.

More than a year went by. He came and went as he pleased. For a while he troubled his mind with justifications, but none was required of him. He and Ruth were leading separate lives now. They would go for days, seeing each other only at mealtimes when, as like as not, she would set a single place for him and he would eat alone. The baby, Clara, had got old enough to care for him, and often he would linger at the table after a meal, holding her on his lap. He would bring in curiosities for her out of the fields—nuts or seeds or birds' eggs or small stones—and she loved to rummage his pockets for them. "What do you have in your pocket, Papa? Let me see, now." It would never be in the same pocket as the day before. Sometimes she had to hunt and hunt. Sometimes even *he* could not find it, and then they both had to hunt; he would be terribly bewildered then—where did it go?—and she would laugh. And at last the treasure would be found and he would get up and put on his hat and leave. Between him and Ruth lay the peace of distance and silence.

Spring came again, and passed, and summer came. And then, on an evening shortly after the longest day, when he set out to visit Rose, Ruth walked from the house and stood in the driveway ahead of him. He slowed his horse and walked him up to her and stopped.

"Where are you going?" She asked in such a way that he knew she knew.

For a moment the question angered him. "You've made that none of your business, my girl," he thought. And then he sensed the pain in her that the stance and look of her defied, and he grieved for her. He saw that his infidelity had touched her as his love had not, that she who could not abide his passion now helplessly and deeply bore his wound. It turned her toward him, revealed her to him, too late, too late, and for no mercy or denial that was in his power—that beautiful woman with her gray eyes, so fine. And he said with a gentleness that she had not stirred in his voice for a long time: "I'm going to look at a red calf with a white tip on the end of its tail." And he said: "You look fine this evening, Ruth."

She turned quickly to hide what her face could not help but show. And he rode on, bearing, in the fierce justice of their bond, the wound he had given her.

After that he was torn. He felt the insult and shame that he had given Ruth, and he felt it, he knew, because he cared for her, because he would be forever yearning and grieving after the loss of what perhaps they never could have had. And with Rose too he was beginning to feel an incompleteness. His love for her led to nothing, could lead to nothing. As long as he might come to her he would come, however welcome, as a guest. It was as though he bore for these two women the two halves of an irreparably divided love. With Ruth, his work had led to no good love. With Rose, his love led to no work. With Rose he had come within the gates of Eden, but had found there no possibility for a worldly faith or labor. With Ruth he had made an earthly troth and travail that bore no delight; they had lost the vision of their paradise. Now when he rode away from home, he felt Ruth's hurt and accusing eyes at his back, and he accepted their blame. When he entered the cottage garden and came away he felt more and more the futility and uselessness of being out of place; there was nothing at all that he could do to justify or redeem or safeguard Rose's gift.

"You're *free* here," she says to him. "You owe me nothing."

She says: "*Give* me? You give me what I give you—what we'd waste by keeping." She laughs.

He is sitting with his feet on the hearth, his hands held to the blaze. It is a cold night and he is warming himself, getting ready to leave.

"You're letting me use you," he says.

She is standing beside him, her back to the fire, looking down at him. They are self-consciously not touching, the inevitable parting before them, sorrow between them.

"Don't you know you deserve better?"

And then she does touch him. She touches her fingers to the side of his face, though she does not bend. "I'm getting what I've *asked* for," she says. "I have this because I don't want anything else, that I can have."

But she is lonely for him. She wants what she cannot ask and he cannot give. He sees it in her eyes. It makes a sorrow in him that only his grave will heal.

Three years went by, and more. February came again, and he sent his tobacco crop to Louisville and went down on the steamboat to see it sold. He was detained there and did not start home until the fourth day. His boat left the city nearer midnight than morning, and all day breasted the muddy Ohio under a gray mist. In mid-afternoon when the boat tied up at the landing at Hargrave a number of people from Port William came aboard. When they saw him a hush came over them and they looked away. And then one of them—a dignified little man with a gray mustache, a man of jokes and riddles and precisions of speech—divided himself from the group and came over to the railing where Jack stood. He was watching the roustabouts unload several boxes and barrels of cargo.

"Ah. You have been away," he said. And his eyes were on Jack, not with their usual humor or subtle mockery, but with care, for he had a heavy story to tell, and he was perhaps curious and perhaps a little afraid.

"Yes. Four days."

"Ah. Well, we have had quite a tragedy at home since you have been away. Mrs. McInnis was burned to death. We buried her yesterday."

Jack said nothing. The little man went on, his voice carefully implying that both he and his hearer had a certain disinterest in the matter. "It's thought that she was standing on the hearth and her skirt somehow touched the blaze. She ran out in the yard, and so saved herself from burning with the house. But by then, of course, it didn't matter."

He ceased speaking and stood for a time in silence beside Jack. It was a duty he had assumed, not to let mere chance bear the news, and he was troubled and wearied by what he had done.

And then, with perhaps a greater effort than before, he broke the decorum to which he had so far been faithful. "Jack," he said, "I'm sorry."

Jack did not answer. He had not moved. There was no visible change in him, except that his eyes, which had been attentive to the activity along the wharf, were now not looking at anything. The little man stood responsibly beside him a few moments longer, and then he went away.

Now Jack is riding up the hill road toward town, he is riding up out of the river valley toward the height of his desolation and his grief. He has begun a silence that he must keep forever. It is as if the muddy river behind him, and the road, and the stones of the road, and the trees, and the town ahead of him, all have lost their names. And he is a stranger in that place, nameless and without words.

When he comes to the graveyard he turns in between the stone pillars of the gate and climbs to the height of ground where the stones stand mute in the wind beneath the bending cedars. He finds the raw, freshly mounded grave beside the grassed and sunken one of the old doctor.

It is true. Though he makes no sound, the air around him seems suddenly full of crying. He does not move from the saddle. He sits still. For a long time no thought or word comes to him to define or name the wound of the new grave. There above the town, among the stones, in the wind that draws steadily through the limbs of the cedars, he sits on his horse and does not move.

The wind is steady and strong, bearing the sky of gray clouds swiftly eastward. The sound of it broods upon the country as constant as silence. The town is shut against it, silent within it.

Dusk comes, bringing the darkness up like rising water. The horizon draws in. The wind sighs in hidden distances. In the town pale lights have begun to show in windows. And finally Rose returns to his mind. Now he can see her again as she was. The wetness of tears is on his face and he mourns for her—her quickness, her free giving, her grace, gone from the world. He recovers the thought and the touch of her, and he knows her, silent and still where she lies.

At last he touches his heel to the horse's flank and turns him to the wind. Once they are in the road again, headed home, the horse quickens his gait, eager for the barn. When, days later they pass again the blackened remains of the little house, the sprangle of the ruined elm stiff against the last light, they do not stop.

Now he returns to the daylight, to the bench there in the town flooded and foundering in the brilliant sky—driven, a trembling refugee, out of the past by old grief too sharp to bear. He rises from the bench and starts up the street in the direction of the hotel. And now the street sways under him. The town tilts like a sinking ship, poised upon darkness. A veil covers it.

He hears a voice calling to him: "Uncle?" He opens his eyes. "Uncle?" A young fellow he does not know is bending over, looking down at him. "Uncle, are you all right?"

Seven : Through the Valley

Andy Catlett knows more than he understands, and more than he *will* understand for a good many years to come. He has too much on his mind and in his nature, too many choices, in too complex a time, to permit him to be close to any clarifying insight.

He has grown up in Hargrave, the county seat, a little town looking up and down the Ohio at Cincinnati and Louisville, dreaming of distance and money and bright lights, uneasy about its failure to attract the notice of Progress, sniffing with some contempt and some embarrassment—for fear, perhaps, of being familiarly recognized—in the presence of the farmers on whose custom it has depended since its beginnings; and yet half content, for the time being, to be self-contained and small, perched like a pretty memory on the outside sweep of the river's bend, in love with summer evenings when the merchants and the office men and the distillery workers come home to shady yards and the smells of supper, in love with foggy mornings when the towboats whistle and groan in the river's blind shroud, summoning the wakers to the mysterious and the far. And Andy knows that life. In the confines of church and school he learned the truths to which the town pretended or aspired. In the countenances and characters of his teachers, in long back yard rambles home from school, in Saturday afternoon adventures in alleys and outskirts and along the river, he learned how the truths fared in daily life.

But Andy's family had its roots in the farmland around Port William—

Wheeler, his father, is in a sense not so much a lawyer as a farmer who practices law—and the boy has grown up also under the eyes and hands of Mat and Margaret Feltner, his mother's parents, of his father's parents, Marcellus and Dorie Catlett, of Elton and Mary Penn and the Coulters, and of Old Jack Beechum, his great-great-uncle. And so, though he knows the town, he knows as well truths older than the town's truths; he knows a faith and a hardship and a delight older than the town's ambition to be a bigger town. Since the beginning of his consciousness he has felt over and around him the regard of that fellowship of kinsmen and friends, watching him, warning him, correcting him, teasing him, instructing him, not so much because of any ambition they have for him as because of where he comes from and because in him they see, come back again, traits and features of dead men and women they loved.

Andy remembers his father's parents, Marce and Dorie Catlett, now dead, who left to Wheeler, their only surviving son, the good farm on the Birds Branch Road which had borne their name for three generations. He remembers the threadbare life of that couple—the unadorned, sparely furnished rooms of the house; fences and buildings patched and repatched; old Marce's worn and carefully kept and mended tools. He remembers how, after Dorie's death, the house yielded parcels of letters, canceled checks, paid and canceled promissory notes and mortgages, all neatly tied with strips of rag, and drawers full of neatly bound bundles of cloth scraps, remnants of thread and string wound around folds of paper, boxes of buttons clipped from worn-out clothes. As long as Andy knew them, though they had no dependent then and were safe from the ruin that they had struggled against, it was still characteristic that Marce should wear a straw hat neatly patched with pieces of various old shirts; that Dorie's dishpan should have its leaks stopped with tiny bits of rag; that her oven door should be propped shut with a tobacco stick and a rock. And before he was old enough to be told, Andy had already glimpsed the aim of that pinching thrift and hard saving: that the farm should survive them undiminished and unencumbered, that what they had served should go on. He remembers the vacancy of the house after his grandmother Catlett's death. The place was sharecropped then by the Coulters—Marce Catlett was a first cousin to Dave Coulter, Burley and Jarrat's father—and by Elton Penn, Old Jack's tenant and, by then, as much his son as any man would ever be. And Wheeler would be there, looking after things, before he went to the office in the morning, or before he went home in the evening, or both.

And so it was only to be expected that from the time they were old enough to stay away from home Andy and his younger brother, Henry, would have an aspiration toward Port William. They would go there whenever they could—to visit with grandparents, to eat big meals that dependably included dishes they especially liked, to tag along with the men when they went to the fields, to drive the teams to the field and hold the reins while the men loaded the wagons, to pick berries along the edges of the woods in the dewy mornings, to gather walnuts and hickory nuts on bright Saturdays in October, to ride horseback to the ponds to swim, to fish in the river or the old quarry, to listen to the stories that Mat or Burley or Old Jack would tell, not always when asked, but when the mood was on them. While they were still only children, Andy and Henry became initiates of a way of life that was threatened and nearly done with in that part of the country, and of which they would be among the last survivors.

When the two boys became old enough to work it was only to be expected that they would go to work in the fields that their kinsmen for generations before them had gone to work in, and that the men who had been their friends and at times their playmates would then become their exemplars and taskmasters. For Andy this was a time of trial that put him in touch with the depths of his pride and endurance. It set the first standard in his mind that he recognized as worthy of his effort. From that company of men, that brotherhood of friends and kinsmen, his teachers, he glimpsed a vision of human possibility that would not leave him.

They were hard enough on him. They did not spare him. He was a skinny, clumsy boy, and embarrassed about it, and they did not spare him even that.

Burley would squeeze his leg above the knee, delicately, as if in wonder. "Andy," he would say, "does your leg swell up like that *ever'* summer?"

"Sixteen years old," Elton Penn said. "Boy, it's *time* you learned to set up by yourself."

And they would tell him: "Come on, Andy! Come on! Come on!"

They would stand and watch him fumbling, coming up with his end of it. "Hundred dollars waitin' on a dime."

But at the end of a long day, when he had lasted and done well, he felt their satisfaction with him, their relief and pleasure.

"Tired, old boy?" they would ask him.

"No," he would say.

And then maybe one of them would lay an open hand on his head, or give him a clap on the shoulder or a hug.

And now he is getting ready to leave that place and life that have made him what he is. He is going to bring that old life, familiar to him as though he has known it for generations, to the test of what he does not know: a strange city, books and voices that will be a new world to him. Through the summer he gave little thought to this coming change. As always, there were the long workdays in the fields, an occasional day or two of fishing and camping by himself along the river, and nights at Hargrave with Kirby when they went to a dance or a party or a show or sat talking and loving on the hilltop above the town and the meeting of the two rivers. He let the time go by.

It was only a week ago, when Henry left Port William and went back to Hargrave to begin his own last year of high school, that Andy felt himself borne irrevocably toward the future that is so dark and questionable to him. He stayed on with Mat and Margaret, working in the tobacco harvest, but now there lay in him a strange sorrow that seemed not to go away even when he was thoughtless of it or asleep. And when he put his mind to it he knew what it was: it was fear that in order to be what he might become he would have to cease to be what he had been, he would have to turn away from that place to which his flesh and his thoughts and his devotion belonged. For it was the assumption of much of his schooling, it was in the attitude of most of his teachers and schoolmates, it was in the bearing of history toward such places as Port William and even Hargrave, that achievement, success, all worthy hope lay elsewhere, in cities, in places of economic growth and power; it was assumed that a man must put away his origin as a childish thing.

One morning, unable to sleep, he got up before daylight and slipped out of the house. He went through the barn lot and down the hill under the stars and through the gathering strands and shelves of mist, and past the house where the Berlews were asleep, and into the woods of the hollow—a way familiar to him since as a boy he first followed Joe Banion hunting. Once in the woods he could see very little, only strange, faint, and shifting clouds of light here and there, but he was on a path that he knew and now he walked slowly. The darkness was close around him; he felt the touch of it. A strand of spiderweb broke wet on his face. He went on down into the depth of the woods, a place where two forks of the little stream joined. The stream was dry; only the tireless, endless songs of the crickets flowed and glimmered in the air. Around him the trees stood still; not a breeze or a breath was stirring. Ahead of him he could hear a bird begin to sing, a voice solitary and strong greeting the first light. He waited, standing still as the trees, until the growing morning began to reach in through the leaves and he could see a little, and then he crossed the bed of the stream and climbed up through the woods on the other side, angling down the hollow as he went. He came shortly to a broad, gently sloping bench that lay between the wooded slope he had just climbed and an even steeper one above. Here the trees had been cut down, leaving a clearing of perhaps two acres. Now through the rim of low bushes that edged the clearing he could see a brightening expanse of sky.

He had come into one of the deepest depths of his memory. One morning when he was only three or four years old, when this clearing stood planted in tobacco, ripe for harvest, he had come here with Mat, and Joe Banion, now dead, and Virgil, longer dead than Joe. They came down on a wagon drawn by a team of mules, one black and one, in her old age, nearly as white as snow. He remembers the early morning sunlight slanting in, the dew shining, the hummingbirds at the tobacco blooms, the solemn quiet of the woods. The clarity of that morning hour and the freshness of his eyes mythified the place, so that now it seems to him that he came there first, not fifteen years ago, but generations ago beyond memory—that when Mat and Joe and Virgil brought him there is was not new to him, but more familiar than his own flesh, and the place and the hour held him like his mother's lap.

He stepped out through the wet foliage into the edge of the clearing and stood still. In the snag of a deadened tree near the center the bird continued to sing. Though Andy would not realize it until later, he was no longer thinking. The place filled his consciousness; amply and easily it woke within his mind, and his mind rested in it. For some time as he stood there, so quieted that he was hardly aware of his own presence, the only sounds were the bird's song and the constant dreaming song of the crickets. And then off in the woods, where he would not go again for a long time, he heard a squirrel's teeth grate into the rind of a hickory nut; and he could see again ahead of him the intent gray figure of Joe Banion. Joe's black hand moved from under the brim of the dew-beaded felt hat where it had been resting meditatively against his face; his hand rose and opened in the air, alert as a deer's ear. Quietly, that hand still in the air, Joe looked back to warn him with a stern shake of his head—*Don't make a sound!*—and stepped off slowly along the edge of the woods, his silent feet brushing a dark track through the dewy grass. The black man and the small white boy gone out of sight, Andy stood some moments longer, recovering the presence of the place, and then he turned and went silently back into the woods.

Now his last day in the field has come and gone. He was cutting with Nathan and Elton when Mat and the other Coulters and Lightning came back with the wagons to load again. They stopped at the far end of the field.

"Andy," Mat called. "Time for you to be going, I expect." He knew that Andy had some getting ready to do and some good-bys to say and a date for that night, and he did not want him to be rushed.

The three cutters had just finished their rows and were standing at the end of the field, resting, not talking much now, for they were tired.

"All right," Andy called back.

"Well, old boy, are you going?" Elton said.

"I guess so."

"Well, Andy," Nathan said, "be good and be careful."

"Yeah," Elton said, "mainly be careful. And we'll be seeing you back in these parts before too long, I expect."

Andy put his tools down beside the water jug at the row end. "Yeah." He was looking off into the river valley, and then he looked at his friends and held his hand out. They shook, and said good-by.

The others were already loading the first of the wagons, Mat building the load, Mary Penn on the tractor, the rest on the ground. When he passed them they did not stop, but raised their hands to him.

"So long, son," Mat said.

He left the field and from some distance looked back, and there they were, going on, intent upon their work as before, and the ripe tobacco and the evening light surrounded them with a glow that would stay in his mind, he thought, forever.

At the house Little Margaret and Mattie were out playing in the yard, and he knew that Hannah had come back to tell him good-by. He washed his hands and went into the kitchen to find her sitting with Margaret at the table. In the chair beside her Margaret had a pile of neatly folded laundry and a large paper sack. She was obviously waiting for him, with a lot she had been keeping on her mind to tell him.

"Now," she said, beginning without a greeting as she was apt to do when her mind was much occupied, "here are your extra clothes. They're clean, and I've just darned your socks. And that sack's got your shaving things in it and some other odds and ends. And there's a check in there from your grandaddy, for your wages, and I think maybe a little more."

"Okay," Andy said, picking up the bundles. "Thanks." He was beginning to be upset, wanting to hurry and be gone.

"Now wait," Margaret said. "I'm not finished." And she resumed the list she had been keeping in her mind. "Inside that sack is a tin with some cookies in it for you to take with you to school. Don't shake 'em around and make crumbs out of 'em, and don't eat 'em before you get there. And when you do get there I want you to apply yourself and study hard, because I think you've been given a good mind and it would be a shame to waste it. Your grandaddy thinks so too."

Margaret paused, searching out and ordering the rest of what she had to say. Andy stood holding his bundles, grinning, for he knew he would have to wait until she had said it all. This way his gentle grandmother had of being duty-bound and stern amused him. And yet as never before he was touched by her. She was thinking more than she was saying or was going to say. Her eyes were on him, gentle and grave behind her glasses, and as if she deliberately held him he could not look away.

"Listen," she said. "There are some of us here who love you mighty well and respect you and think you're fine. There may be times when you'll need to think of that. And before you leave Port William I think you ought to go over to the hotel and say good-by to your uncle Jack."

"I will," Andy said. "I was going to."

"And that's mainly all I wanted to tell you. Now come here and kiss your old granny good-by."

Andy went obediently and leaned down and kissed her. "Good-by," he said. "I'd better go."

"You'd better," Hannah said. "It's getting late." She stood and put her arms around him. "You'll have to clean up before you kiss Kirby, but I'm going to kiss you the way you are." And she kissed his cheek. "Be good, hon," she said, and turned him and pushed him toward the door.

And now it seems to him it is all behind him: the day, the summer, his life as it has been up to now and as he knows it. Margaret and Hannah have made him feel it, this sudden great division. Margaret's words have made an occasion of his departure; that, he will realize later, was her gift to him. She has reached deeply into him, into that luminous landscape of his mind where the past lives, where all of them—some who are now dead—are together, and where they will all still be together long after many of those now living will be dead. She has shaken him out of what might have been the simplicity of his leaving and has made it as complex as it really is, as she would have it be. And so as he leaves the house Andy steps out into a changed and strangely radiant world, for he is walking now not merely in the place but in his knowledge of it, surrounded by the ghosts and presences of the ones who have cared for him and watched over him there all his life, and he is accompanied by earlier versions of himself that he has lived beyond. The ache of an exultant sorrow is in his throat.

He puts his bundles in on the seat of Mat's truck, which he will drive home and which Henry will bring back after school on Friday, when he comes to rejoin the tobacco cutting. Little Margaret and Mattie have followed him out across the yard.

"Good-by, kids," Andy says.

"I want to go," Mattie says.

"You *can't* go, dummy!" his sister tells him.

"I want to go, Andy."

"Next time," Andy says.

"Good-by, Andy," Little Margaret says. "Come back smart."

As Andy leaves the truck and starts out toward the street he can see Old Jack sitting alone in one of the chairs on the hotel porch. The old man sits so still that he appears inanimate. Even from that distance it is clear that he is not conscious of where he is; he is not *present* there. Yet, as he crosses the road, Andy is aware as always that he approaches a past much older than his own, that he cannot remember. But it is a past that, listening to Old Jack's and his grandparents' talk, he can enter with his imagination, and in that way he has taken possession of it. Since boyhood he has been Old Jack's listener, the student of his memory. And there has come to be a part of his mind that is spacious and old, hung with the elaborately interconnecting web of Port William lineages, containing landscapes changed beyond recognition years before his birth, peopled by men and women and children whose names have turned mossy on their graves.

He steps up onto the edge of the porch and with contrived cheer greets the old man's vacant body. "How are you, Uncle Jack?"

And still for many seconds Old Jack's mind stays wherever it has gone. The intelligence of his eyes remains distant and he does not move. And then he turns his head and his eyes light and look up. "Why, son," he says, "I'm all right now. I thank you." And he waves his hand in a gracious gesture of dismissal, for he thinks that Andy is the young fellow, now two hours gone, who helped him back to the porch after he fell there in front of Burgess's store. But this voice sounds more familiar and dear to him than that one.

"Who is it?" he says.

"It's Andy Catlett," Andy says. And then, he adds: "Wheeler's boy."

"Good God Amighty!" Old Jack says. "Honey, I didn't know you." And he shakes his head in chagrin, and says again: "I didn't know you."

For a moment he feels sinking through him a sort of shame in having failed to recognize the boy, for whom his love was prepared far back in his love for Ben Feltner. It occurs to him that he probably will not live much longer, and he thinks: "All right. All right."

"I'm glad you came, son," he says. "Come here where I can get ahold of you."

Andy steps up within reach, and the old man stretches out his right hand and feels the boy's arm from the shoulder down to the wrist, and then he runs his hand down his leg from hip to calf, grasping and pressing, as he once would have handled a horse's leg. He says as he always says: "Son, you're mighty nar' in the hams." He shakes his head. He has been hoping the boy would muscle up some.

For Andy these examinations are both funny and embarrassing, and yet peculiarly moving, for he recognizes a sort of loving-kindness in them. He submits to them at a considerable sacrifice of dignity—something, it seems to him, he can hardly spare.

Old Jack lifts his hand from the back of Andy's knee and takes hold of his elbow and pushes him away a step. He leans back now to regard him. There is something about Andy's brow and eyes that reminds Old Jack of Mat and, before Mat, of Ben. Aside from that, he looks mainly like Wheeler. He has the strong nose that Wheeler got from his father. Old Jack snorts with pleasure, a stockman's pleasure, at seeing a good trait passed on. He touches the boy with the point of his cane.

"You're your daddy made over," he says. "You're Wheeler Catlett made over. But you'll never make a lawyer like your daddy. You ain't got the head for it."

And he continues for a while to gaze upon the boy. He is not sure what this boy may make of himself. The other boy, that Henry, will make the lawyer. This one, this Andy, with the eagerness to know of the old times, his interest in the men who have worked the fields, is a puzzle.

"What're you aiming to make out of yourself?" He prods the boy gently again with the end of the cane.

"I don't know."

"God Amighty," Old Jack says.

"A farmer, I guess," Andy says doubtfully. A farmer is what he would *like* to be. But now he seems to be headed away from that.

"Well," Old Jack says, also doubtfully. "You can be that."

"Books," he thinks. The boy loves books. Reading books is something Old Jack has done little enough of in his day, the Lord knows. He read in his readers while he went to school and has forgotten all that, except for the mouse that gnawed the rope and turned the lion loose. And long back, Nancy used to make him read some in the Bible. But that was a tedious and difficult labor—to take a little book in his hands and say over all those black words; it seemed to him you could go on doing that forever, and he found it a worrisome prospect. Marvelous, to him, the sort of mind that could look at words and see through them to what they were about. He could seldom do it. The Twenty-third Psalm, he could see through that one. He has read the newspaper some, but he either cannot see through those words at all, or he sees not people but little things hopping around like fleas.

But suddenly he remembers his manners. Here he is sitting in the most comfortable chair, and the boy is still standing. He leans and hooks his cane onto a rung of an old kitchen chair that sits nearby, and draws it over.

"Here," he says. "Set here."

"No," Andy says, embarrassed again. "Here. I'll take this other one."

But Old Jack has already begun getting up. He hauls himself up by one of the porch posts and then lets himself down again, with as much difficulty, into the kitchen chair. He clangs his cane across the seat of the metal armchair he has just abandoned. "Set down!"

Andy obeys with relief. Now maybe they will talk. That is a comfort that Andy has hoped for: to sit there on the porch, the town before them, the legendry of its past near them, himself, for the moment, only a welcome and beloved presence of the present. How many times have they sat there, Old Jack remembering and meditating on his memories; Andy listening, his mind slowly illuminating a country of the past that, by Old Jack's gift, he was born to, though he does not remember it. But that is not going to happen today. It will not happen again.

Old Jack taps his cane on Andy's knee. "You've just come from the tobacco patch."

"Yes sir."

"What were they doing?"

"Nathan and Elton were cutting. Grandaddy and the others were loading."

Old Jack is sitting on the seat of the chair without leaning against the back—straight up, like a rider. He taps the boy's knee lightly with the cane; he leans forward a little. "Now tell me, son. Who was cutting in the lead?"

"Elton."

"Ah!" Old Jack says. He leans back now. He would have had it so.

In the rhythms of that difficult work Elton moves like a dancer, seemingly without effort, lightly. Old Jack can see him. In his mind he can see him very well indeed: swaying, bending and rising in the ripe row in the rich evening light—that unsparing man, so careful in his ways—his blade striking lightly as he bends, the golden plants turning to rest upon the stick, the row lengthening rapidly behind him, shortening ahead of him. With increasing distance the figure loses personality; it becomes a lyrical embodiment of youth and strength and grace, of the passion to achieve what the light allows. It could be Elton or Nathan, or Mat in his day, or Old Jack himself in his, or any of that crop of young men, strong and swift, eager in their spending, who have risen and flourished and fallen in this place, generation after generation.

And now Old Jack's eyes are those of a man intently watching, though he looks at nothing within the range of sight. For some time Andy gazes at his face, wondering at him.

But the silence draws out to unusual length, and Andy's mind, burdened with such a press of subjects, wanders away from Old Jack. He begins to think of the coming night, for that too has been much in his thoughts. It will be his last night with Kirby for he does not know how long, maybe until Christmas. Kirby, who has been the lure and trial of his thoughts for more than a year, also will be going away to college, but she will be going to a fashionable Eastern school, in keeping with her social aspirations. The thought of this division of their ways saddens Andy and bewilders him and fills him with the confusion of unacknowledged resentment. And yet he has an eagerness for this parting; he hopes that it will clarify the bond between them in a way that will ease his mind. He wants this love to be easing to his mind, and it never has been. He wants Kirby's love to be an unconditional gift—as he believes his love for her to be—and Kirby is most formidably equipped with conditions. She might *not* love him forever, she will declare. How do they know? They are both young, she reminds him, as if she has managed by some imperturbable womanly insight to be as doubtful and prudent as the old. And not his most passionate declaration can entirely divert her from her concern for proprieties and clothes and points of etiquette. The fact, which neither of them can yet admit, is that they belong to different worlds:

Andy to the fields and woods of Port William; Kirby to the close and ambitious circle of the first families of Hargrave and to the world beyond. Not only does Andy suffer this difference without understanding; he adores Kirby all the more because of it. It is as though all the contradictions of his time and place and nature would be resolved in him if Kirby would only love him as he is. But she will not do it. She loves him as raw material.

That Andy is sufficiently raw even he knows. At parties, depending on who is there, he is apt to be either impossibly shy or offensively loud. He is suspicious or contemptuous of strangers, disrespectful of shrines and verities, stubborn, surly, intemperate, and generally extreme. All this conflict and confusion is a salt water of exile across which he sees what he takes to be his heart's destined homeland flowing with milk and honey: Kirby, so lithe and smooth and lovely, so gently gazing upon him when he has managed to please her, so blessedly quenching, bright and clear above all confusion. No wonder he is confused.

For a while, as he sits in silence with Old Jack, thoughts and griefs, fantasies and hopes as customary as ritual occupy his mind. But the changing light distracts him. He looks at his watch and stands. He will have to get on his way.

Old Jack slowly turns and looks up at him, the tall, gangly boy standing there with the gum and dirt and sweat of the tobacco patch on him. It is Wheeler's oldest boy, Andy. "Son, I'm glad to see you. How're your folks?"

"All right, and I'm glad to see you too," Andy says. "I've got to go now."

Old Jack takes hold of his forearm. He holds him there, looking up at him. There is something troubling that he knows about this boy. He cannot remember what it is.

And suddenly Andy understands the bewilderment in the old man's face. He senses the deep forgetfulness that is coming over him, the present more and more a series of unjoined moments from which he takes shelter in the firm sequence of the past. He has forgotten what happened earlier today, the conversation at dinner, even Andy's arrival a few minutes ago.

"I'm going away to school," Andy says. "I'm going to leave in the morning."

"Up there to the college," Old Jack says.

Andy nods.

Old Jack holds to Andy's arm, looking intently up into his face. What lies ahead of this boy? Where will this departure lead him? What will he have to face? What strength is in him for the work he will have to do? He sees that he has come to an end in this boy. When Andy Catlett turns and leaves he will step away into a future that Old Jack does not know and that he cannot imagine.

His eyes blur. Though the boy is standing there, he cannot see him now. And he has turned him loose. His hand is opened and raised in benediction and farewell. "Learn your books," he says. He means more than that, but that is what he says again: "Learn your books."

There are three quick steps across the boards of the porch, and the boy is gone.

For a moment Old Jack feels unsupported, as though he might fall one way or another out of the chair. That passes. He recognizes himself again. He is as he is and as he has been, remaining after departure and after taking away. He knows that as one of the inescapable themes of his life: the departure from him, from the beginning, of men and women he has loved, of days and years, of lightness and swiftness and strength. The other theme is faithfulness to what has remained. What has remained is the good darkness out of which all things come, even the light, and to which they all go back again. Too little respect is paid to that now, he thinks, but he has respected it. He has thought of it without ceasing. It has been the center of his mind. By that he has endured and come through. He has not looked back from it or dreamed of an easier way. Having put his foot into the furrow, he has not looked back, though he has known that it must deepen into a grave.

Coming through took him a long time: from the stillbirth of his and Ruth's son in the February of 1893 until a day in the early spring of 1908 when he finally got out of debt for the second time. Fifteen years, and the shadow of death was heavy on him all that time. That was his labor for longer than Jacob labored for the daughters of Laban, and the last five of those years were the darkest and the worst.

In the years following Rose McInnis's death he labored in darkness. In his memory of them they have neither color nor brightness. It seems to him that in all that time he did not see the sky. He worked from dark until dark; to carry on the necessary trading and to deal with his creditors he rode to town at night when he could not work. He drove and deprived himself, he spared himself nothing. Whenever possible he spared Ruth and Clara. For himself, he did not ask the cost. He suffered whatever was necessary to earn the dollars that his creditors and his own honesty required of him. He no longer had a vision to lighten and justify his toil. He hoped for little; for days and weeks together he did not hope at all. He was dull and enduring and strong as a beast of burden, and he took a certain grim satisfaction in that. He went on because he would not stop, because it was not thinkable that he would quit or ease himself or look away from his task. And always near him was the thought of the dead woman who had loved him as he was, and of the living one who could not.

The shadow of that time returns to him again and fills his mind. He bears it again. Though he has not moved, though he still sits on the porch as Andy left him, he has gone back into his old darkness, his eyes veiled with the sorrow of a man who must bear his own weight through the world as a burden. And yet it is not now as it was then, for ahead of him in his thought he is aware of the presence of Mat Feltner. Now his memory urges him forward. He would like to see Mat again as he was when he was a young man.

When he finally got clear of his debt to the bank—he had already paid what he owed to Ben Feltner—it was one of those days of false spring in late February, a day of clearing after rain, the shadows of clouds sliding over the country as fast, nearly, as a horse could run. He worked through the morning, and as soon as dinner was over rode to town with the check for his tobacco crop that he had sold the day before. He went into the bank and endorsed and deposited the check, and wrote out another in payment in full of the interest and the remainder of the principal, and received the canceled mortgage in his hand.

"Well," the cashier said, as if to begin some goodhearted tribute, for he knew of Jack's hardship. But Jack was already walking to the door; the old urging and haste were still upon him, and there was work he had to do. He folded the mortgage, creasing it twice, and put it in his shirt pocket and got on his horse.

It was a good black horse that Jack had named Socks because all four of his pasterns were white. Used to his rider's haste, the horse went into a canter without a touch or a word as soon as he felt him mounted, and carried him swiftly out of the town. It was an easy, tireless canter that black horse had, and Jack rode with the unconscious grace that for years still to come would turn heads in the street

Sitting on the hotel porch, erect in the straight chair, he feels again the motion of that canter—pleased, now as then, by the horse's fidelity to his gaits. And yet he is virtually thoughtless, the gray wheeltrack flowing backward beneath the unvarying beat of the shod hooves. It has been a long time since he has looked forward with his old free delight in the use of his mind; his thought has been freighted with necessities and urgencies, bound by the limits of present time and season and weather. And yet, now, he is aware of change, as a man preoccupied might be aware of the weather changing above his head. His life has changed; another hinge has turned. And after they have turned into the Birds Branch Road toward home he slows the horse to a walk, the better to think of it.

He touches the folded mortgage in his pocket; his fingertips press upon the crisp edges of that paper that had pledged him to the loss of everything and bound so many years of his labor to the fear of ruin; with his thumb he feels the flatness and smoothness of the paper, affirming the reality of that death pledge, now broken. After so long a time he is free. And the farm is free. He names in defiance and triumph the names of those who thought him beaten. But his words to himself are without strength, as though repeated from memory, and his deliverance remains unreal. Still, he rides along with a strange alertness, looking eagerly around him, as though his eyesight has been freed from a long confinement.

At the top of the rise beyond the ford on Birds Branch he comes in sight of the upland fields of his own place: the house and outbuildings and barns, the winter-deadened sod of the pastures, the veil of green wheat over last year's croplands, the gray stone of the fences bending along the contour of the slopes, the trunks and the webbed and spiked branches of the unleafed woods. And now it seems to him that his soul breaks open, like a dull coal, shattering brilliance around him. He has been gone but little more than two hours, and yet he returns as from a long voyage or a war. Now he does consciously feel the open sky above him, the eye of heaven clear upon him. In that long, unwearying gaze he feels the clarity of his outline. Over his farm in the distance the broad cloud shadows pass, darkening and leaving bright again the rinsed air.

Clear and whole before him now he sees the object of his faith as he has not seen it for fifteen years. And he feels opening in himself the stillness of a mown field, such a peace as he has never known. For the last five years he has lived at the limit of his strength, not looking up from the ground, perishing at night into lonely sleep as though his bed was a grave from which he rose again in the dark, sore in his bones, to take up again the labor of repaying the past. And now, the shudder of realization in his flesh, he sees that he has come through. He has been faithful to his land, through all its yearly changes from maiden to mother, the bride and wife and widow of men like himself since the world began.

He lost his life—fifteen years that he had thought would be, and ought to have been, the best and the most abundant; those are gone from the earth, lost in disappointment and grief and darkness and work without hope, and now he is only where he was when he began. But that is enough, and more. He is returning home—not only to the place but to the possibility and promise that he once saw in it, and now, as not before, to the understanding that that is enough. After such grievous spending, enough, more than enough, remains. There is more. He lost his life, and now he has found it again.

Words come to him: "Yea, though I walk through the valley of the shadow of death . . . Yea, though I walk through the valley of the shadow of death, I will fear no evil"—the words of the old psalm that Nancy had made him repeat when he was a boy until he would remember it all his life. He had always been able to see through those words to what they were about. He could see the green pastures and the still waters and the shepherd bringing the sheep down out of the hills in the evening to drink. It comes to him that he never understood them before, but that he does now. The man who first spoke the psalm had been driven to the limit, he had seen his ruin, he had felt in the weight of his own flesh the substantiality of his death and the measure of his despair. He knew that his origin was in nothing that he or any man had done, and that he could do nothing sufficient to his needs. And he looked finally beyond those limits and saw the world still there, potent and abounding, as it would be whether he lived or died, worthy of his life and work and faith. He saw that he would be distinguished not by what he was or anything that he might become but by what he served. Beyond him was the peace and rest and joy that he desired. Beyond the limits of a man's strength or intelligence or desire or hope or faith, there is more. The cup runs over. While a man lies asleep in exhaustion and despair, helpless as a child, the soft rain falls, the trees leaf, the seed sprouts in the planted field. And when he knows that he lives by a bounty not his own, though his ruin lies behind him and again ahead of him, he will be at peace, for he has seen what is worthy.

Jack stopped the horse when he first reached the height of ground, and he stood him there as though to be observed by a critical eye—not consciously, he was not thinking about the horse, but that was the habit of his hand. And now he starts him on again, slowly so as to continue his thoughts and to savor the completion of his return. It seems to him that his life has come to its true beginning. He is forty-eight years old.

That his life was renewed, that he had been driven down to the bedrock of his own place in the world and his own truth and had stood again, that a profound peace and trust had come to him out of his suffering and his solitude, and that this peace would abide with him to the end of his days—all this he knew in the quiet of his heart and kept to himself. Who, in those days, could he have told? Not Ruth, for hers was a different faith, and no hardship or joy of hers would be apt to bring her nearer home; anyhow, he and Ruth did not speak of matters of importance. Not Clara; Clara was still only a little child—in a sense she would remain a child, for she would never be tasked with a burden that would teach her what he knew. To Ben perhaps, but Ben was old, and what Jack had to tell bore too strict a qualification of pain to be told to a man so near the grave and so much beloved. But it seemed to him that Ben already knew it, for when he told him that he was out of debt and on his feet again, Ben smiled and said: "Then it's all right, Jack my boy. Didn't I tell you so?"

It was only to Mat, after Mat had reached his manhood, after he had received the inheritance of Ben's land and proved worthy of it, that Jack began to speak out of the exultant knowledge that had come to him. Then, fearing that Mat would look away from what he had undertaken or attempt in too much pride to go beyond it, Jack would gesture with his hand to the ridges and hollows that bore indelibly for them both the memory and the mark of Ben, and he would say: "That's all you've got, Mat. It's your only choice. It's all you can have; whatever you try to gain somewhere else, you'll lose here." And then, taking hold of Mat's shoulder, letting him see in his eyes with what fear and joy he meant it, he would say: "And it's enough. It's more than enough." And he would quote that psalm: "Yea, though I walk through the valley of the shadow of death, I will fear no evil: for thou art with me; thy rod and thy staff they comfort me. Thou preparest a table before me in the presence of mine enemies: thou anointest my head with oil; my cup runneth over." He would ask as if half in jest: "Do you understand that, Mat? Do you know what it means ?" And he would put his eye on the younger man in order to keep him from saying glibly or too soon that he understood. And so he saw to it that when the time came when Mat had need of them he too would have those words in mind.

The renewal of his life made no change in the look of him or in his ways. By then he was determined and hardened; outwardly he had become what he was to be. From then on only time would change him. His hands and face and body were marked by his years of work and exposure; their shape and attitude were fixed as though his flesh had been annealed to the toughness of wood or live bone. And there was about him an air of stubbornness and withstanding; it was in the way he stood and moved, in the set of his face, in the directness of his stare.

Anyone who looked at him in those days sensed that he was a man who would do unflinchingly whatever he thought necessary, whatever affection or loyalty or obligation demanded. He had become a man whose presence changed other men; when he came among them his influence was discernible in the way they looked or stood or spoke.

But however little change there was in his aspect and his ways, the inward change was deep and permanent, and where this change was made visible was in his place. Coming home that February afternoon after he had paid his debt, he saw that under the oppression of his darkness and his long struggle the farm had grown stark. The yard trees standing nearest the house had died or grown too infirm to be trusted to stand, and had been cut down and not replaced, leaving the house without shade. The orchard that his father had planted had nearly died out. The buildings all needed paint. The new barn that he had built ten years before to replace the burned one never had been painted; now the boards had turned gray and were streaked with rust from the nailheads. Most troubling of all were the two or three of his fields that under the constraint of his debt he had neglected or overtaxed. Wherever he looked he saw the need for remedies and repairs, and he felt the satisfaction he would take in those attentions.

He remembered what he had understood after his fight with Will Wells: that he could not ask another man to work without hope; that therefore he would not acquire more land, but instead turn his effort with redoubled care in upon the land that was rightfully his, not because it belonged to him so much as because, by the expenditure of history and work, he belonged to it, and because he could properly attend to it by himself. The onset of that understanding had been the immediate cause of much of his hardship. Now it set him free. Its results slowly became visible around him and under his feet. His thoughts no longer ranged the distances of possibility but were contained inside the boundaries of his farm. He became again the true husband of his land. He still worked and went ahead as before, but now his work was healing; it restored the health of his place and his own satisfaction. He had come a long way from what he might have been. Now as he drove to the field in the morning and returned again at night, as he looked after his stock in the pastures, and made his rounds of the pens and barns, doing his chores, there was a joy deep in him, shining, reflecting the sky, like water in a well.

He began the restoration of his fields. As he had time and money he repaired and painted or whitewashed the buildings. He planted young shade trees in the yard and fruit trees in the orchard, and carried water to them in the dry spells of summer. He planted berry beds and an arbor of grapes, hedges and edgings and shrubs. Under his hands the place became abundant and beautiful as it had never been in the time of his memory.

He saw in Ruth's face certain softenings of pleasure at what he had done. He knew that he was making her life more agreeable, and he was glad. But such acknowledgment as she made she might have made to a stranger. He expected no more. It was too late, and he accepted that. But he felt keenly the want of words between them. If they could have spoken with some candor of themselves, with some mutual pleasure of their place in the world, looking ahead with concern or with hope, that would have made them both different lives and different deaths. But she could not offer, and he could not ask. That was his failure: he had not united farm and household and marriage bed, and he could not. For him that was not to be, though the vision of what he had lost survived in his knowledge of his failure, and taught him the magnitude of his tragedy, and made him whole. It was too late for a woman's love. And that was all that was lacking.

He is aware, in the cold, of the dark barn, the smells of hay and dung and the bodies of animals; the sounds of chewing, of hay drawn from mangers, of corn rattling in troughs. The mangers are full of hay, the stalls and pens fresh bedded. The north wind sings in the gable. His fingers and toes ache with the cold; he is hungry and tired. The work done, he can think of sleep. For a moment the apprehension of sleep comes powerfully over him, seeming to sway him in his tracks, the thought of the released weight of his body and its repose.

He goes out and draws the doors to behind him and turns to the winter twilight, the cold wind bending close over the farm out of the starless distance. The ground is whitening with snow, and he can feel the flakes melting on his cheek. For some moments yet he stands still upon the turning world, in the whirl of the snow, in the falling night. Closing the doors against the cold dark, he has closed and cherished in his mind the thriving that the barn holds, the vision of that harbored life emerging in green spring. This is his devotion. He tilts his face up into the long fall of the snow.

Again he thinks of Mat, ahead of him, but near.

In the summer of 1912 Ben Feltner died—he was killed, shot down in the road by a man whose friend he had been. Old Jack feels again the weight of that sudden grief.

Now, with Ben gone, Jack had his mind, and his eye too, on Mat. He had loved Mat through all his growing up and had had the satisfaction of seeing him become a young man worthy, perhaps, of his father. He kept that *perhaps* in mind, for he knew that the test had not come, and he waited for the test.

The test came, he knew, with Ben's death, and it would not soon end. Knowing the lonely responsibility that Ben's absence would make for Mat, he began spending more time on the Feltner place than he had before. When he could spare a half day or a day, he would get on his horse or take a team and go to Mat's, and just step into whatever work was going on. He gave Mat his help; more important, he gave him his presence. As thirty years before Ben had been on hand for him, so now he was on hand for Mat. He gave him the steadiness, and he gave him the little uneasiness and the pressure, that a young man can only get from an older man's knowing eye. It was one of the good fortunes of his life that when Mat needed him he was in the clear, for then the time of his solitude was ended.

Now he can see Mat again as he was when he was twenty-seven or twenty-eight years old—a little flighty yet, a little too impatient, a little too easily upset or discouraged, but a good man, and the time was coming when the two of them would speak and work together as equals. He can see Mat's face as it was then: big ears that stuck out, nose a little hooked like the Beechums' noses, his father's clear, understanding eyes, hat tilted jauntily onto the back of his head; a grin—maybe a little uneasy, maybe a little defiant—turns up the corners of his mouth as he watches Jack's eyes for some sign of what he thinks.

And again Old Jack raises and opens his hand.

Eight : Exile

Mrs. Hendrick has already stepped twice from the kitchen to the screen door and called sharply *"Supper!"* and though Old Jack heard her both times he instantly forgot. Or rather that crisp command fell upon the current of his thought like a dry leaf on the surface of a deeply flowing stream, to be borne forty years away. It is not until she deigns to come out onto the porch and stand before him, arms akimbo, that her summons penetrates the half-lit closet of his present consciousness, and she has the satisfaction of seeing him look up at her, his eyes deeply shaded and withdrawn beneath the bill of his old cap.

"Good evening, Suzy."

"Supper's ready. I already called you twice."

"I thank you. I'm a coming."

To make sure of him this time she waits until he has stood and then she follows him in through the door and across the diminutive lobby and into the dining room, where the rest of the derelict company—four old women and two other old men—are waiting.

It has been many years since Mrs. Hendrick's hotel has had a guest in the usual sense. The roads have long been too good and the means of transportation too swift for any self-respecting traveler or politician or salesman to have been benighted at any such out-of-the-way place as Port William. And it has no doubt been even longer since any self-respecting wayfarer would have looked with relief or favor upon the accommodations afforded by the frugal Mrs. Hendrick. The hotel's clients these days are permanent residents—that is, of course, within the limits of mortality. It is understood that they will be there until they die, or until they are carried away to die in a harness of tubes in some hospital bed, for they are the ancient widows and widowers of the neighborhood, too old or infirm to remain alone in their isolated farmhouses, either childless or unwilling or unable or uninvited to move in with their children who have gone off to jobs in the city. Their fate is to perish at modest rent under the care of Mrs. Hendrick, who, to give her due credit, does keep them warm and well fed, and who does keep a responsible eye on them. For years now Jayber Crow has referred to the establishment as the local airport: "Where are gathered those about to depart into the heavens."

Under the eye of the ever-watchful Mrs. Hendrick, Old Jack goes to his accustomed place at the end of the one of the long tables that is occupied, the three others being bare. Thinking to remove neither his coat nor his cap, he sits down in his chair at the angle at which he has drawn it out from the table, and he keeps his left hand gripped onto the crook of his cane. His attitude thus communicates a most tentative and passing relation to the table and the assembled company. He appears ready at any second to rise and be on his way.

When the evening's bowl of soup is placed before him he first pays no attention to it at all, and then, the sounds and motions of the others' eating seeming to remind him, he begins absently to skim the broth off the top and convey it to his mouth, holding the end of the handle of the spoon tremulously between his thumb and forefinger. All this is observed by Mrs. Hendrick, for usually he addresses himself as straightforwardly to his supper as to whatever else demands his attention; usually he eats heartily and asks for more. She watches him closely, perhaps anxiously, perhaps even with sympathy, for she is not a heartless woman, though by her lights her relationship with Old Jack has not been rewarding.

"Are you all right, Mr. Beechum? Do you feel all right?"

"I'm fine. I thank you, Suzy."

"Is there something else I can bring you?"

"No. No. I thank you, good woman."

Their relationship, from her point of view at least, has been difficult. Old Jack's character and habits and values and hours have in no way conformed to hers. He would be up, wanting breakfast, in what she considered the middle of the night. When she sought to be mild he would be uproarious. Where she was discreet he was blunt. Where she was modest he was oblivious. Where she was pious he was profane. And so on. For three or four years after he came to live there he oppressed her with a huge garden to which, without asking, he sacrificed her whole back lot. She had to admit that it was a saving and even a pleasure to have the vegetables that he grew at no cost to her. But to have them hove down by bushels at odd hours and without warning into the middle of her kitchen floor, to be nearly buried under them, to be called out of bed, along with her female boarders, four hours after midnight with the expectation that they would then and there commence canning several bushels of tomatoes—it was too much, and she was glad when it ended. It did end, of course, as in her calmer moments she knew it would. For in what she has perhaps had to consider her contest with Old Jack, time has been on her side. And the nearer she has come to triumph the more indulgent and sympathetic she has afforded to be. They have managed to live together under the same roof as long as eight years because, on his side, Old Jack has been largely oblivious of their contest and, on hers, Mrs. Hendrick has been constrained to balance her troubles with his rent.

Old Jack has thought of his residence there as merely an arrangement, an accommodation of his circumstances, in itself neither good nor bad. Or perhaps he thought it the best of bad alternatives. The worst alternative would have been to go to live with Clara and her husband, the banker Gladston Pettit, in their luxurious house down in Louisville, where in his judgment he would have been not only old and useless but hopelessly a stranger.

In choosing to go to live the last of his days in the hotel in Port William, Old Jack acted upon what he took to be two indisputable truths: that if he no longer belonged on his farm—if, living alone there, he had become a source of worry to his friends and kin—then at least he still belonged among the people he loved and knew well; and that Clara was his daughter only in name and, in some sad and irremediable way, in affection.

From the time of her birth Clara was Ruth's child. He always knew that. He felt a sort of moral inferiority in the matter, having failed to be the man Ruth wanted him to be, and so he yielded in this, as he did so far as his means and his pride would allow in all matters of the household. Besides, unless the child had followed him to the fields, which she rarely even wanted to do, he could not have hoped to influence the growth of her character. And so she grew up in the house, under the persistent tutelage of her mother's thwarted ambition. He foresaw early the way it was fated to go—well enough at least that he was not surprised at the way it went.

When she completed such education as was afforded by the one-room school on Birds Branch, Clara was sent away during the school term to a seminary for young ladies then flourishing at Acropolis, a town a few miles up the Ohio above Hargrave. And when she finished her courses at Acropolis she attended a small church college in central Kentucky. Though he was out of debt by the time Clara enrolled at Acropolis, Jack was by no means well off, and during the eight years that she spent away at school he was again forced to skimp and deny himself in order to pay her expenses. In the warm months he often worked without a hat or shoes. When he plowed his corn he frequently went bare-legged to keep the blades from fretting the cloth of his pants. No economy was too petty or too harsh for him, and by such measures he gave Clara her education. And Ruth was as self-denying and as frugal as he was. She saved and used every crumb and scrap and rag. She made Clara's dresses. She sold cream and eggs so that the girl would have pin money. Clara emerged at the age of twenty-two—a pretty, bright-eyed, happy, and eminently marriageable young lady—out of the hardship and the bitter division of her parents, as innocent of any real knowledge at least of the hardship as if she had been the wealthiest of her schoolmates.

Clara spent the first two years after her graduation from college in a series of visits back and forth with her now-scattered friends. It was a long season of courtships and marriages. The old house was brightened up for another of its eminent occasions; this time it adorned itself for the final departure of its last blood heir. But until the day of that departure came, the house was lively as it had not been in his memory. Parties of young people would visit for days at a time. There would be great flurries and excitements of dressing and getting ready; there was eating and laughing and singing; the dust-covered automobiles of young men would be parked under the trees in the yard. The work of the farm went on as if far in the background now, Jack a solitary figure in the landscape.

Sometimes when she was at home alone Clara would invoke again their old half-sly comradeship of the time of her childhood when he would come in from the field with surprises for her hidden in his pockets, and he would listen, smiling, while she prated of events and people of no meaning to him. He would be again the remote, gentle man she remembered from what seemed to her a long time ago. But she was not a child now, and she could not speak to him as she was. He knew that he bore in her eyes also something of the strangeness and hardness, the implicit threat or danger, that Ruth saw in him. In the presence of her friends she covered him with the urban stereotype of the farmer: the man of the soil, the hardy plowman, rugged and proud, but somewhat comical in his speech and old clothes, with his quaint preoccupations and his stay-at-home ways. "Oh, Papa, you're *impossible*," she would say, "*just* impossible." He saw it all, and knew what it meant.

Their estrangement was sealed forever by her marriage to one of the automobile drivers, Gladston Pettit of Louisville, a young man of some considerable attainment already, with brilliant prospects in banking and finance. They had the wedding at the house—an affair that embarrassed Jack by its multitude of formalities and by what seemed to him its ostentation, and saddened him by its gravity and finality. And this was Ruth's triumph. She had done as she would have been done by.

Glad Pettit was a man of extraordinary good looks, as he well knew, with his athlete's build, his regular features, his disarming, confident smile, and his wavy hair parted straight in the middle. He bore toward his father-in-law all the blandishments and observances of a generalized and perfunctory respect. Whenever Jack said anything Glad listened with what he deemed an excess of attention. He inquired, with a large show of interest and in as much detail as the hearsay of his knowledge would allow, about the goings on of the farm. For Glad Pettit was affability itself, and to him, as to Clara, Jack was the Man of the Soil. He loved to confide to his colleagues in the city that men like his father-in-law were the salt of the earth. But however much he admired the type, Glad was no more inclined to learn about it than he was to emulate it. His shoes were as innocent of the earth as a pair of newborn babes.

On their Sunday visits to the farm, which would occur about once a month, Clara and Glad would arrive in Glad's automobile, which seemed year by year to grow larger and richer and brighter, its immaculate gloss bearing like an insult the dust of the country roads. During the time of his and Clara's courtship Glad had always parked under a tree at some distance from the house, but now he drove to the very foot of the porch steps so that Clara could pass from the car into the house almost without touching the ground. She would go out to the kitchen, where her mother, just back from church, with an apron over her best dress, would be preparing dinner. And Glad, carrying in the Sunday paper, which he always brought to bestow upon his in-laws, would sit down in the rocker in the living room and cross his legs and light a cigar and read. When Jack came in Glad would rise, shake his hand, enact his ritual of interest in crops and weather, and resume his paper and cigar.

And always, when they left, the car would be loaded with the bounty of the farm. When the young people were getting ready to go Ruth and Jack would always be gathering up for them whatever was in season, from the first greens of the spring to the last turnips and parsnips of the fall, from the frying chickens of early summer to the turkey at Thanksgiving to the cured ham at Christmas. And in this again Jack felt his estrangement from them, and he sensed that Ruth did also. For what could their simple and hard-earned abundance mean to that beautiful, carefree pair who made such an unabashed show of needing nothing? The car loaded, the Pettits having gained its sanctuary again in their still immaculate shoes, Jack and Ruth would stand in front of the porch and watch them out of sight.

That all of this followed unerringly the line of the old breakage and division in his life, Jack knew. He knew that the shape of his undoing had entered the door of his house and feasted at his table. Perhaps he did not yet foresee in those Sunday dinners the solitary meals that he eats now among strangers in the exile of his old age. But these suppers at the hotel too often recall his memory to that bounty of smokehouse and henhouse and garden carried off in the banker's gleaming machine to the satisfaction of such hunger as might be roused by the balancing of figures in a book.

He remains half-turned from the table, looking away. The bowl of soup, still unfinished, sits forgotten at his elbow. The others are starting on their pie. As though under a tangible weight of his silence, they have spoken little during the meal. And now at intervals they glance covertly at him and look away and glance at him again, for his right hand has begun to beat upon the corner of the table a rhythm as slow and unregarded and implacable as the ticking of a big clock. He is thinking of finality, the inescapability of finality. He sees in that marriage of Clara's, that shiny car rocking and gliding almost soundlessly away over the bumps of the drive, the permanence, the final insignia, of the failure of his own marriage.

It ended in the failure it began in. He was seventy-five years old, and Ruth was sixty-four. It was April and he was plowing; though slower and less agile than he had been, he was still a vigorous and a strong man. The sun gleamed on the young grass. He was plowing an old bluegrass sod, and it broke well, the furrow crumbling as it turned, dark to light. With deep pleasure, with his familiar sense of the blessedness of that old return, he watched the earth roll dark off the moldboard and settle and lie still again in the long, straight furrow. At noon he watered and stabled and fed his team. He hung his cap on its nail on the back porch and stepped into the kitchen to find no one there and the stove cold.

He stands in the door a minute, only looking, a cool cell of fear opening low in his throat. And then he hurries through the back hall to the living room, and finds Ruth lying on the sofa, struggling for breath.

"I'm sick, Jack. I can hardly breathe."

She has been stricken for several hours. She is nearly exhausted by her suffering, and the distraction of fear is in her eyes.

"Don't talk," he says. "It'll be all right."

He brings down a quilt and covers her and builds up the fire and goes.

He never rode such a ride again—an absolute demanding in his hands, the gathering and springing of the horse's stride beneath him, the road reeling back.

By luck, he found the doctor in town, and started him on his way. He then turned his lathered horse up the street toward Mat's. Mat had eaten dinner by that time and gone back to the field, but Margaret said she would send for him, that she would phone Clara, that she and Mat would come straight on as soon as he got to the house.

The doctor and Mat and Margaret and two neighbor women stayed through the afternoon and night. It was clear that Ruth had had a serious heart attack, that she might not recover. They watched by her bed until morning, and then Mat went back to town and called Clara again as they had arranged.

And shortly after noon that day Clara and Gladston Pettit, who were weathering the Depression in their accustomed style, drove into the driveway, followed this time by an ambulance. Weeping, Clara leaned over the bed and kissed her mother. "My dear," she said, "we are going to take you home with us, where you can be comfortable."

She might have said a better thing. She might have put it a kinder way for the sake of the ones there who had done the best they could. But what she said left nothing for them to say.

Now Jack stands at the door, holding it open to permit the men of the ambulance to carry Ruth out. Her face is white and drawn, and her hair is gray on the pillow, and her good gray eyes are weary and unresisting even to death. The bearers hesitate a moment, turning out the door, and Ruth reaches and takes Jack's hand. Their eyes meet as though a great deal might be said now, were there time.

"Jack," she says. "Bless you, Jack. Good-by."

They carry her on. They slide the stretcher into the ambulance. Clara gets in beside her mother. The attendants shut the door and get in themselves. Glad Pettit waves to those on the porch and gets into his car. And then the two vehicles ease out, smoothly rocking, over the stones of the drive.

He goes back to his plowing, for that is what there is to do. But he remembers her hand that perhaps had never touched him so—the feel of her hand, its passing lightness, age's loosening of the skin upon the delicate bone. He remembers her eyes, their tiredness, their unaccustomed gentleness upon him, as though wearied at last into some final and frail, hopeless and helpless love. He walks in the furrow, following his plow, an old man, white-haired, yielding his steps to their immutable finality. He knows the finality of life and time, of loss and grief. He knows the permanence of failure. His body is shaken now by cries that come strange to the ears of his team, and his tears fall into the furrow as it opens.

The sound of his cry alerts him only momentarily to the ranked pairs of old eyes along the two sides of the table, turned toward him in their various lights of alarm and amusement and concern. And then he turns from them again, passes them by, and goes back, as if his chair is a speeding vehicle swerving out of the past and into it again. There is no longer enough here to hold him.

Mat and Margaret or Wheeler and Bess Catlett would take him down on Sunday afternoons to the Pettits' house, where Ruth lay dying in a sunny room, always attended by a nurse. He would sit, mainly silent, in that many-windowed room, while the others talked. It seemed to him that he understood little of what they said there, and he said to himself that he must be getting old. When he came in, and again when he left, Ruth would rouse out of her stillness and look at him and take his hand. Even the pain had somehow gone out of that; it had become a sort of duty. The old division between them had now been substantiated by real distance. Ruth was already in another world.

And each time Jack came he brought them the gifts of his faithful work: baskets of eggs, baskets of whatever was in season in the garden, a jar of cream, a joint of pork. That was what he had left for them in the way of speech. It was his message to them. Had it come to different people it might have been eloquent. In the circumstances, it was muteness itself, the helpless gesture of their estrangement. It would be dressed by the Pettits' yardman, prepared by their cook, served by their maid. It was good food, such stuff as Glad Pettit could have purchased by the ton if he had wanted to. It might as well have been purchased.

They brought what this world had left of Ruth Beechum back to Port William to be buried in the September of that year. And it was not long after the funeral that Jack made his one direct attempt to influence his son-in-law. He realized after Ruth's departure that Clara no longer had a tie with her old home. *He* and Clara certainly had little enough in common. As things were, there was little that they could do for each other.

And so he cast about in a final, desperate attempt to make between them a common ground and a bond.

One of the farms next to his was for sale, and he knew, or he had good reason to suppose, that Glad had the necessary cash. And that set him thinking. To begin with, he was getting old, and he was worried by the thought that his own good farm would be inherited by the Pettits, who knew nothing and perhaps cared nothing about it. But if they would buy the adjoining farm *now*, then maybe he would live long enough to teach them what they would need to know. It bothered him that they had no child to have the land after them, but he thought he had no right to consider that; if his own daughter could only take some comfort from and give some care to the place that he had served all his life, then that would be enough. He had visions of the kindness and the mutual pleasure that might follow Glad's purchase of that farm. For Jack it would make possible a generosity that had not been possible before. It would allow him to do something for Clara and Glad that no one else would do as well. In their absence he would look after their place for them. When they came out on Sundays, he could show them what was going on. He would find various ways of instructing them, so that when he was dead they would be able to carry on for themselves. One day, he thought, they might want to come there to live. For had he not heard Glad already talking about what he might do when he retired? Retirement seemed to him a rather objectionable ambition—but then that was not his business. Or, he thought, suppose Clara should be left a widow. Then she could come back here and have the security and comfort of her own place, with her own people around her, with Mat and Wheeler to look after her.

And so one Sunday afternoon Jack showed Glad the farm and told him what he had on his mind, or most of it. Glad was no longer the lean and muscular young man he had been when he married. He was fleshy now and somewhat stooped in the shoulders; he had been more weakened by the last fifteen years than Jack had been by the last fifty. But his superfluous weight, covered as it was by a tailored suit, set off by his graying hair, a diamond ring, and an excellent cigar, somehow made him look richer, more substantial, more dignified than ever. As his consort, Clara had become plump and opulent. Though she was still pretty, her looks had somehow become merely decorative. She had made of herself a sort of portable occasion for the ostentatious gifts of her husband, a sort of bodiless apparition in fine clothes—useless, so far as Jack could tell, for either work or love.

"There it is," Jack told him. "You can have it, I think, at a good price. You can take care of it and make it a satisfaction to you. And it'll be there when you need it."

Even as he spoke he realized how little pleased he was by the vision he was conjuring up. He disliked the idea of a man *retiring* to a farm. He disliked the idea of a man living on land that he thought himself too good to dirty his hands in. So far as he was concerned, a man who thought he was better than such dirt as he and Glad had underneath their feet that Sunday was a good deal worse.

As Jack should have known, Glad did not buy the farm. He did not refuse, of course. He agreed with everything Jack said with his usual readiness and affability. That Jack had thought of him and Clara with such kindness was something he appreciated very much, he said. But he did not buy the farm, and he never mentioned it again. And with that avoided subject between them, Jack and the Pettits had less than ever to say to each other. From then on Clara was more likely than not to drive out alone to perform those observances of daughterhood that she felt to be her duty, and to take back as always a load of eatables "fresh from the farm," as she and Glad liked to say to their guests at dinner.

What he had done, Jack realized, was make a good plan and then invent a man to go with it. What he had imagined had certainly had no relation to any possibility that was in Glad Pettit. He was long past the hopelessly defiant anger that might once have led him to rebuke or accuse. Though he knew that Glad's show of interest in that farm that he never intended to buy amounted to condescension and insult, he said nothing. As had come to be his way, he merely accepted that his daughter and son-in-law were of a kind that was estranged and alien, and probably inimical, to his kind. A man without a place that he respects, he thought, may do *anything* with money.

He never spoke of it except once, about a year later, when he told the story to Mat.

"I've hated to tell you that," he said. "I dislike to talk against my own. I tell you to show you the kind of man you're not, and to give you some idea what it's worth to me that you're the man you are."

Jack touched Mat then, to give his words the direct weight and warmth of his hand. They were sitting, talking, on the bed of a wagon in Mat's barn lot, looking out over the ridges to where the river valley opened. And Mat understood that what Jack had said was both a confession of great failure and an affirmation of what had not failed, meant to clarify their kinship in its final terms.

"It wasn't the *buying* that stopped him," Jack said. "He'll *buy* damn near anything—and then sell it as soon as he can get more than he paid. It wasn't the buying. It was buying it and then keeping it and taking care of it, with me here where he'd have to look me in the face—that's what stopped him.

"I know him. I know what's in him. He don't want to take care of anything outside of figures in a book. He wants to lend money to people to make worthless things and buy worthless things. Worth would put him to too much trouble."

And then, after a long silence, looking away, he let it go. He grinned. His big hand came down heavy on Mat's shoulder. "Bank stock don't eat grass, Mat—and nothing eats bank stock."

He never had called Glad Pettit by name—they were too different, too distant from each other, for that. He had called him "son" or "young fellow." Now, in the silence that followed their Sunday talk about the farm, he took to calling him "Irvin." Clara hastened to attribute that to her father's "childishness." But Mat knew what it was. Jack was an old man, but he was as clear as ever, and in his clarity more direct; he had renamed Glad Pettit to signify that he was *done* with him.

At about the same time he also withdrew, bluntly and finally, from all other relationships that had no meaning to him. He granted no more worth to mere formality or blood tie; he would no longer stir a foot for old time's sake. Now when departed relatives or old acquaintances would return from the cities they had gone off to and come by his place for a nostalgic visit, he would get out of sight if he saw them coming in time, or he would go on with his work and leave them standing. He would not be mussed and reminisced over as a relic of somebody else's past. Much less would he indulge their hints of how greatly they had improved themselves, or listen while they exclaimed over the difficulty of his work, implying their superiority to it. They belonged to another world, and he could expect nothing from them. He would be faithful to what he belonged to: to his own place in the world and his neighborhood, to the handful of men who shared his faith. He had taken his final stand. He would accept no comfort that was not true.

For nine years after Ruth's death he stayed on by himself in the old house. He found it necessary to rent out his tobacco crop, but he continued to carry on the rest of the work himself. And now he did his own cooking and washing, and mended his clothes after the fashion that he liked to describe to Mat as "middling rough." He slept as before in his room in the back of the upstairs, and did the rest of his household living in the kitchen. The other rooms he seldom entered, and they remained as they were. Occasionally Clara would come out with her maid and clean the house, sweeping and dusting and airing it out. When he left finally in 1944 to move to town, the six rooms in the fore part of the house, except for the perceptible dulling of disuse, looked exactly as Ruth had left them. But more than ever he kept away from the house. So far as necessity and the weather allowed, he stayed in the fields or at the barn. There was a history in those places that was not tragic, and that comforted him. From the house that for him would always keep in it the old stirrings of loss and grief, breakage and failure, he would go back to the farm itself in which, given the simple condition of his care, all was as it had been. Sometimes now when he sat, "studying" as he would say, in the door of the barn or at the edge of a field, he would have the attitude, Mat thought, of an old dog who hears something alive stirring and breathing deep in the ground.

And then that ended. At first it was Clara's idea that he should come to Louisville and live with Glad and herself. There was no use in talking about that. But the awareness deepened in him that he had become a worry not just to Clara, which he doubted anyway, but to Wheeler and to Mat. He saw that they were driving out to his place a lot oftener than they should have, given the work they had to do. And so when Wheeler finally suggested, as a sort of compromise, that he move into the hotel in

Port William, Old Jack's resistance was only a token of principle, and it did not last long. On the day he moved to town Elton and Mary Penn moved into the house to be the farm's first tenants—to prove, to Old Jack's surprise, worthy of his trust, and to earn his love.

And so here he is, alone at the supper table in the dining room of the hotel. The other boarders have finished the meal and are gathered in the small lobby, watching the wrestlers on television. He does not know that they are gone. He does not hear the crowd cheering the feats of Chief Don Eagle and Argentina Rocca. Mrs. Hendrick has been around the table half a dozen times, carrying off the dishes, gathering the soiled paper napkins, brushing away the crumbs, but he has not been aware of her, nor does he hear the dishes clattering now in her dishpan. He is getting on in his thoughts to the end.

When he moved to town he knew the last of his life's hinges had turned. It seemed to him then that he was finished. Because he had no descendant of both mind and blood, his own descent had become wayward; it had led him out of his homeland into exile. Having no longer the immediate demands of his place and work to occupy his mind, he began to go into the past. His place and his life lay in his mind like a book and what is written in it, and he became its scholar. His thoughts went back to his place and moved obsessively over it, whether in the pleasure of familiarity or in the pain of old reminding. His mind was formed long before the days when maps were commonplace, and even longer before the time of aerial views and photographs. His memory of his place was never overlooking and abstract, but ground-level, as immediate always to his hand as to his eye. It was unified in his mind not by the geographical relationships of its various boundaries and landmarks but by his old routes over it, its aspects opening ahead of him as he ascended heights of the ground or emerged from trees, moving over it in his memory, on horseback or behind a team or on foot.

"Don't you want to go in there and watch the TV?" Mrs. Hendrick asks.

He shakes his head. "No," he thinks. "God Amighty, no." For the cost of living beyond his time is in putting up with the various noises and contraptions of these new times, this modern ignorance, as he has come to call it in his mind. The modern ignorance is in people's assumption that they can outsmart their own nature. It is in the arrogance that will

believe nothing it cannot prove, and respect nothing it cannot understand, and value nothing it cannot sell. The eyes can look only one way,
and Old Jack believes in the existence of what he is not looking at and
what he does not see. The *next* hard time is just as real to him as the last,
and so is the next blessing. The new ignorance is the same as the old,
only less aware that ignorance is what it is. It is less humble, more foolish
and frivolous, more dangerous. A man, Old Jack thinks, has no choice
but to be ignorant, but he does not have to be a fool. He can know his
place, and he can stay in it and be faithful.

That a whole roomful of people should sit with their mouths open
like a nest of young birds, peering into a picture box the invariable message of which is the desirability of Something Else or Someplace Else;
that a government should tax its people in order to make a bomb powerful enough to blow up the world; that a whole country would attempt a
civilization with the exclusive aim of getting out of work—all that is
strange to him, unreal; he might have slept long and waked in a land of
talking monkeys. He is troubled and angered in his mind to think that
people would aspire to do as little as possible, no better than they are
made to do it, for more pay than they are worth, as if the old world were
destroyed and a new one created by Gladston Pettit.

Mrs. Hendrick has turned out the kitchen light, and now she stands at
his elbow again. "I'm done here and I want to turn the light off. Want me
to help you up?"

Hastening ahead of that, he pulls himself to his feet. But the effort is
too sudden. Vertigo blinds him and he staggers. He feels Mrs. Hendrick
strongly holding him by the arm. His vision clears and the swinging
room steadies and rights itself.

"Are you all right now?"

He nods, but she continues to hold to him as he starts out of the room.

"I thank you, Suzy. I can make it now."

He pats her hand and she lets him go. Watching him, she stands by
the light switch, and turns it off as he leaves the room. He crosses the
lobby through the commotion of the TV and sets foot into the gloom of
the corridor, heading for the room that the landlady insisted he take
when it seemed to her that he had grown too feeble to manage the stairs.
It has never suited him. He likes to sleep upstairs.

He walks with the effort of a man burdened, a man carrying a great bale or a barrel, who has carried it too far but has not yet found a place convenient to set it down. Once he could carry twice this weight. Now half would be too much.

Nine : Return

Now he feels ahead of him a quietness that he hastens toward. It seems to him that if he does not hasten, his weight will bear him down before he gets there. He reaches the door to his room and opens it. The room is in the back of the building, looking out on the fields that lie close against the little town. No town lights shine in the window, but he does not turn the switch; there is a moon and that makes light enough—more than he needs.

He goes slowly across the room to his chair, an old high-backed wooden rocker that sits squarely facing the window. This is his outpost, his lookout. Here he has sat in the dark of the early mornings, waiting for light, and again in the long evenings of midsummer, waiting for the dark. He backs up to the chair, leans, takes hold of the arms, and lets himself down onto the seat. "Ah!" He leans back, letting his shoulders and then his head come to rest.

For some time he sits and looks out, getting his breath, grateful to be still after his effort. And then he rises up in his mind as he was when he was strong. He is walking down from the top of his ridge toward a gate in the rock fence. It is the twilight of a day in the height of summer. The day has been hot and long and hard, and he is tired; his shirt and the band of his hat are still wet with sweat. He can feel the sweat drying on the backs of his hands and on his face. His team has been watered at the pump and put away and fed, and all his chores are done. The day is fin-

ished. He does not know why he is there or where he is going, but he
does not question; it is right that he should be going. A deep hush is
upon everything. Under the slowly darkening sky the countryside has
the sense of surrounding distance that it has only at night. The lives of
the darkness have begun to stir. He lets himself through the gate and fas-
tens it behind him. From there he follows a wagon track that slants down
the face of the slope and enters the woods.

In the woods it is already dark, but he knows the way. He lets himself
easily into the steep descent, feeling the track solid beneath his steps.
The trees lift their canopy silently over his head, a presence of the air.
And now the air opens and lightens ahead of him and he comes out into
the pasture on the slope below.

Here is a great pool of warm still air, dampened by the creek, heavy
with the strong scent of the weeds in the hollows. And here the last of
the light is redoubled, reflected back and forth between the walls of the
little valley so that it brims with radiance. The air seems substantial, as
though a man might step out upon it and walk away over the tops of the
sycamores along the creek. Around the clearing stands the dark woods,
and in its center there is a single walnut tree with a square-built cairn of
stones beside it. The pasture was mowed perhaps three weeks ago and
the new growth has risen green over the fallen stems and leaves. It is a
place he has often thought he would like to go to and rest in and be still.

He turns from the wagon track and goes straight down across the pasture through the glow of the air to the tree. He sits at its root and leans
his back and the back of his head against the trunk. All around him is still
now. And he is still, his hands lying at rest in his lap, and within himself
he is still. He can think of no other place he would want to be. Below
him, among the trees along the creek, he can see a pool of water white
with the reflection of the sky.

Slowly the glow fades from the valley, the sky darkens, the stars appear,
and at last the world is so dark that he can no longer see his legs stretched
out in front of him on the ground or his hands lying in his lap; he has
come to be vision alone, and the sky over him is filled and glittering with
stars. Now he is aware of his fields, the richness of growth in them, their
careful patterns and boundaries. In the dark they drowse around him,
intimate and expectant.

And now, even among them, he feels his mind coming to rest. A cool breath of air drifts down upon him out of the woods, and he hears a stirring of leaves. He no longer sees the stars. His fields drowse and stir like sleepers, borne toward morning.

Now they break free of his demanding and his praise. He feels them loosen from him and go on.

Ten : Mat

When Old Jack was not on hand for breakfast, when the kitchen was seen to bear none of the usual marks he left when he fixed his own, when there was no response to a knock on his door, when he was not to be seen standing anywhere along the street, when he was not to be found in any of his old resting places, then Mrs. Hendrick sent for Mat, and Mat found him, or found what was left of him, sitting in his rocking chair before the window. He looked very natural, very like himself. His eyes were open, staring off, and his mouth too was open, his head raised and tilted back; he looked as though he was poised upon the verge of speech, thinking of what he would say. But the spirit was gone from his eyes. His eyes had become substantial and opaque. He had been dead several hours.

Mat, who had known many deaths, who had foreseen and even hoped for this one, nevertheless felt an onset of grief he did not expect. For only a moment he might have wept, and then the knot of grief in his throat dissolved and spread all through him, taking the shape of his own flesh, so that he seemed illuminated and clarified to himself by this completion of so much that he knew.

"At last," he thought "At last. And so well."

And then those words *at last* took a different and more difficult character in his mind. At last Old Jack was helpless. At last the premises of his independence and the ground of his defiance had been vacated, and now the world would have its way with him. There would be the undertaker and the preacher. There would be Clara and Gladston Pettit. There would be proprieties and usages and considerations and bothers. And all would exact their tribute now upon the passive remnant of Jack Beechum, who had so faithfully maintained and honored his difference from them all.

But it came to Mat that now he was the only one who knew; for the moment Old Jack was dead to no one in the world but him. And Mat turned then and drew the only other chair in the room up beside Old Jack's, and sat down. For a while, for only a little while—Mrs. Hendrick would be waiting to know what he had found—Mat sat with Old Jack in death as he had sat with him in life. For a while he let Old Jack's body be safe and secret there with him. And then he got up and laid his open hand briefly on the dead man's shoulder—that touch of the hand, that welcome or farewell, by which Ben Feltner was bound to Jack, and Jack to Mat, and Mat to his dead son and to his living grandsons—he touched him with that casual and forever binding salute. And then he left him and went out to tell those who must be told.

He told Mrs. Hendrick, who was waiting for him in the little lobby, and who explained that she had felt last night that Mr. Beechum was not well, but she had not realized the poor man was as sick as he must have been. And Mat told her it was all right; there was nothing she could have done.

He did not have to tell Margaret, who was waiting on the walk in front of the house, and who knew from the look of him what he had to tell.

"Sitting up in his chair," he said. "Coat and cap still on."

Margaret nodded. She raised her hand and touched lightly the corner of her eye. It could not have happened better, and they knew that. For some seconds they stood in silence. And then Margaret took hold of his sleeve as if to turn him from what was past toward what must be done.

"You'll have to call Clara."

"Yes. And the undertaker."

And then he was set upon by the stubborn sense of appropriateness that has ruled him or troubled him ever since.

"No," he said. "I'm going to the field and tell them first." And he went to his truck.

The day's work was already well started when he arrived. The five men had cut the first rows and were standing at the end of the patch, smoking and talking. They had drunk from the water jug and set it back in the shade of the long grass in the fence row. He was late, and they turned to look at him, wondering.

As he told them he felt the change. He felt it come over them all, as quiet and complete as a night of snow. A landmark that they all had depended on had fallen, and a strangeness came between them and the country. Their minds had already begun to change and things would no longer be as they had been.

Mat felt the change upon himself. Now he was the oldest, and the longest memory was his. Now between him and the grave stood no other man. From here on he would find the way for himself.

He left them and went back to the house. Margaret had already called Bess and Wheeler. She got up and gave the chair by the phone to Mat.

"They'll be here as soon as they can, Bess said. But it'll be up in the afternoon. Wheeler's in Lexington."

"All right," Mat said. "There's no hurry."

He put on his glasses and looked up the number and dialed the undertaker at Hargrave. It was a strange and a stubborn mood he was in. He was standing guard over Old Jack and over his death. He would not have the outline of that absence blurred or its dimension narrowed. The voice of the gentleman on the other end of the wire was full of solicitude, prepared for death, no matter whose, and Mat propped himself against it. The voice assumed that Mat would be down later to select a coffin and to make the necessary arrangements. Mat thought not. The gentleman would be informed of the arrangements when they were made; as for a coffin, the dead would be well satisfied with whatever was cheapest. And so it went, each exchange followed by a silence in which the gentleman on the other end was perhaps taking notes. The dead, Mat allowed, were noted for their frugality. There was another pause. Margaret had been listening to him, her eyes a shade doubtful of what he was up to. And then she smiled to herself and went away. She would be his ally, and he thought there would be others.

"Oh dear!" Clara said when he phoned her. And then, as if suddenly aware from how far off this summons came, she said, "Oh heavens above!"

She said that she would have to phone Gladston, and that they would be there just as soon as they could, and that she did not know just how soon that would be, and that they would be there in time to make all the necessary arrangements.

That was what Mat was afraid of. He said that he was taking care of the arrangements, that she should not worry about anything, that everything was going to be taken care of properly. And he hung up.

That left the preacher to be dealt with, and Mat wanted to go ahead and get that done, the sooner the better. The situation was simpler now than it was likely to be again. When the Pettits came it would get complex, he was certain of that. He was just starting out the door to hunt up the preacher when he saw that young man heading up the walk—sent, it turned out, by Mrs. Hendrick.

The preacher, Brother Wingfare, was a seminary student only recently established with his new wife in Port William—a pale, slightly plump, impeccable young man, very new to his profession, very eager to please both God and man, a difficulty of which he had not yet encountered either extreme. He began, of course, by saying that though he had not had the privilege of knowing—uh—Mr. Beechum, he was very sorry to learn that he was dead. "But," he said, "the Lord knows of our affliction and is our refuge in the hour of trouble."

"Come in," Mat said. He shook Brother Wingfare's hand and held the screen door open for him. He wanted to like the boy, and felt somehow protective of his eagerness to serve, this shy, pale, painfully polite young fellow, so new and vulnerable, it seemed, to whatever might come next. And yet he was vaguely offended and put out to see him undertake upon any occasion the solemn presumptions of his office.

Mat put his arm around the young fellow's shoulders and led him into the living room.

"Sit down."

Brother Wingfare sat down in the chair that Mat pointed to, a platform rocker to one side of the front window.

Mat sat down in the easy chair, facing the preacher. "Well," he said, "I don't know that you should be sorry. After all, you didn't know him particularly. And it's not a tragedy when a man dies at the end of his life."

Under Mat's gaze Brother Wingfare nodded vigorously in agreement.

"As soon as the undertaker has got his artistry done," Mat said, "we're going to bring Uncle Jack's body here. We want to have the funeral day after tomorrow, in the early afternoon. That'll give his daughter and her husband time to drive out from Louisville, if they don't stay overnight here."

He wanted to set the funeral for the afternoon of the next day at the latest, but he knew he had to be careful.

"We want a simple graveside service, nothing else."

That was not what Brother Wingfare had expected. Mat leaned forward, resting his elbows on his knees, and smiled at him.

"My friend," he said, "I want you to understand this." He considered for a moment and went on. "He was not a churchly man. He was a man of unconfining righteousness. He stuck with us to the end. He never liked a great deal of fussing and formality, and we don't want it imposed on him now. That would be kicking him while he's down, if you know what I mean."

Brother Wingfare either did or did not know what was meant. He did not say. But he was paying attention. He heard something in Mat's voice that did not permit his mind to wander. There was a strange authority in this old man with his white hair, with the dirt of the field on his clothes, who spoke as the younger kinsman of a dead man much older. Nothing in his training at the seminary had prepared him for this. *He* was supposed to be the spiritual authority. But he knew that he was receiving orders. And he was afraid that he was taking orders.

"Here's what we want you to do," Mat said. He got up and went to the desk that stood in a corner of the room and brought back his old Bible and sat down again. "Let me see," he said. He put on his glasses and opened the book across his knees. He wet his thumb and turned the pages. "Write these down," he said. And he spoke the numbers of certain psalms: the Twenty-third, the Twenty-fourth, the Thirty-ninth, the Ninetieth, the Hundred-and-fourth, the Hundred-and-twenty-first.

The preacher wrote them down.

"That's all," Mat said. He compressed his lips and looked over the top of his glasses at the preacher. The book shut with a snap.

"That's all? You don't want a few—uh—*remarks?*"

"That's all," Mat said.

"A prayer at the end?"

But Mat was finished. He folded his glasses and stuck them into his shirt pocket and got up and returned the Bible to its place.

"Well," he said, "smells like we'll be having a bite to eat before long. You'd better stay."

"No. Thank you," Brother Wingfare said, rising. "I must go. When will Mr. Beechum's daughter and son-in-law be here? I should speak to them."

"Sure," Mat said. "They'll be here along in the afternoon. Come back whenever it suits you."

After he had accompanied the preacher to the door, Mat returned to the living room and stood a while in front of the window, smoking and thinking. And then he walked a few restless turns of that room. And then he stood again.

He wanted, in fact, much less of an occasion than he had asked for. He had asked for what he thought he could hope to get. He had heard the sound of his determination ringing in his voice, and it had moved him and clarified him to himself. He had become the defender of the dead.

He heard Mary Penn and then Hannah and the children come into the kitchen. And presently he heard the men on the back porch washing up for dinner. He joined them and washed with them, and they went into the kitchen and ate. After the meal the men went into the living room and rearranged the furniture to make space for Old Jack's coffin. When the others went back to the field, Mat stayed at the house to wait for the Pettits. He bathed and shaved and changed his clothes, and then while the women completed their work in the kitchen he took charge of Mattie, who because of all the excitement had refused to take a nap and as a result, according to his sister, had got cross enough to bite himself.

Mat carried the little boy into the living room and sat down in the rocking chair and told a long story about two boys who went rabbit hunting, and who were never satisfied and were always trying to kill one more rabbit, and while they were trying to get one more rabbit out of a sinkhole their dog ate the rabbits they had already killed, and then they didn't have any. Before the story came to an end Mattie stuck his knuckle in his eye and put his head down on Mat's shoulder. And then Mat rocked him and sang to the heavy beat of the rockers:

Old hound dog
Stole a middlin',
Old hound dog
Stole a middlin',
Old hound dog
Stole a middlin'
Many long years a-go.

The Pettits arrived about two-thirty and Brother Wingfare not long afterward. The air of the house became formal then. Mat and Margaret and Hannah sat with their guests in the living room and made the careful conversation of people who do not know each other well and who are not exactly comfortable with each other. The question of the funeral arrangements came up, as it was bound to do, and Mat quickly said that nobody needed to worry; he and Brother Wingfare had already settled everything. Next to Clara, Mat was, after all, Old Jack's nearest of living kin, he was also a good many years older than Clara, and he had generously volunteered the use of his and Margaret's house for the observances that would precede the burial. Mat erected upon those facts a proprietary claim that would have embarrassed him greatly in different circumstances.

After about two hours they heard an engine whispering in funereal dignity in the yard. It was the hearse, backing up to the front porch. Mat went to the door to hold it open, and the others stood to make way. The undertaker and his assistants wheeled the coffin in on silent rollers, positioned it, opened it, and began arranging about it several baskets of flowers. Margaret and Hannah and the preacher stood back in deference as Clara and Glad approached the open coffin to look upon Old Jack in his death. Mat stayed at the door. He had no love for the undertaker's art. But something calm and assured in the stance of the Pettits alerted his eye. And then he saw the perfection of his defeat.

For the coffin testified to its costliness with the assertive elegance of the Pettits' automobile—a veritable Cadillac of a coffin. Its sedately burnished lid opened upon a spotless drift of white as deep and soft as a summer cloud. Upon that cumulus of eternal ease, Old Jack lay in a dark, richly woven suit, a white shirt and tie. The face raised upon the satin pillow had been stuffed and smoothed to look not as Old Jack had ever looked. Only his hands, which lay in undissembling lifelessness at his sides, bore an indelible resemblance to what they had been. They seemed to have grown with utter incongruity out of the sleeves of the president of a bank.

And now Mat held him only in his mind.

Done with their work for the time being, the undertaker and his men departed. The Pettits, saying they could not stay for supper, left soon afterward, the preacher stepping out the door with them. And then Wheeler and Bess and Henry came. The kitchen table was already filling with various gifts of food brought in by neighbors. Mat went out and did his chores.

When supper was over the townsmen began to come, and presently the living room was full of women, sitting and speaking quietly in little groups. The men sat on the porch or stood on the walk, smoking and, like the women, talking in quiet groups that endlessly gathered and divided with changes of subject.

At about ten o'clock the people began leaving, and they went away one or two at a time. Hannah Coulter and Mary Penn were the last of the women to leave. Bess Catlett and Margaret went to bed then, and the rooms of the house fell quiet. On the porch, at the end of a lapse in the talk, Jayber Crow stood and stretched, a gangling silhouette against the night sky.

"Well," he said, "time will finally make mortals of us all."

And Burley said: "Yes, if we don't die first."

Jayber went down the steps, heading for his lodging over the barbershop. And then the last who were going had gone. Save for Andy Catlett, who had gone off to college and would not be told of Old Jack's death until after the burial, there remained only the little company of men who had known Old Jack best, and whom he had loved: Mat, the Coulter brothers and Nathan, Elton Penn, Wheeler Catlett and his boy Henry.

They moved into the living room and sat there, talking on a while by the light of the one lamp that Mat had left burning on the desk. And then, one by one, those who had worked through the day fell asleep in their chairs. Except for his chores Mat had done no work, and his mind teemed and spun with thoughts. He alone sat awake through all the night while his friends, the living and the dead, slept around him.

When they went to the field the next morning Mat went with them, and though they did not say so they worked that day for Old Jack's sake, honoring him in the familiar, and in what he had honored.

Now that the day is done and supper finished, Mat has cleaned up and come out into the back yard to sit and rest in the quiet before his duties as host will resume. Before long the neighbors will be coming in again, and the Pettits will be arriving from Louisville, perhaps to spend the night. He is not looking forward to that. He is weary from his sleepless night and from his day of work. Through the night and the day he has felt himself near to the most wholehearted curse of his life upon the Pettits and the likes of them and upon the tribe of undertakers. But he has not uttered it, he has not even formed the words in his mind, and he knows that he probably never will. For a great deal that would otherwise be large is small within the silence of Old Jack's voice, that so stayed and comforted Mat all his life. That silence is the most demanding thing he knows now, and he has come out to sit alone in it, to let his thoughts come to rest in it, if they will.

But there seems little hope of that, as he ought to have expected, for almost as soon as he is settled in his chair there comes a roar and then a sustained growl from under the hill, and the Berlews' automobile comes crawling up over the curve of the slope like an enormous beetle. It travels up over the grass of the pasture, honking imperiously at the milk cows to get them out of its way, turns, and stops just outside the door of the barn. The two Berlews get out. Lightning disappears into the barn and appears again with Mat's toolbox. He selects some wrenches and, lying down on his back, crawls under the car. Smoothbore stands and looks around, her hair in pincurls, covered with a scarf tied tightly under her chin. She has a way about her that suggests that if only she could be sure no one is watching she would do something else. Now she turns up a feed bucket and sits on the bottom of it near the car. She lights a cigarette. She sits with her feet apart, her knees together, cigarette held aloft in her right hand, her left hand tugging and smoothing the hem of her skirt. While Lightning works she talks to him, and now and then leans down to peer at him under the side of the car.

"Hey, sweet thing," Lightning says. "Hand me them pliers."

This is the Berlews' evening ritual. Mat should have foreseen it. He might as well have gone to sit in the road. The Berlews are travelers; when they are not going they are getting ready to go. That is the way they will be. In acknowledging that, Mat knows he has come to a limit he has grown too old to assail. But it troubles him. He lets it trouble him.

Once, when Joe Banion and Nettie and Aunt Fanny lived there, the little house where the Berlews live was a living place. Then there was a garden, full of vegetables and flowers. There was a flock of hens and guineas that made their living mainly by foraging in the pastures and the woods. There was a pen with a pig or two to eat the table scraps. The front porch was a forest of potted plants. The rooms of the house were carefully kept, the walls adorned with Aunt Fanny's embroidered hangings and with keepsakes.

The Berlews go there only by necessity, to sleep or to eat. The center of the Berlews' life is the automobile that Lightning now lies under, tinkering at it, as he perpetually must, to keep it running until Saturday night—the "small Packard," as Burley calls it. The car, whose blue-green paint has begun to crack and chip off, leaving irregular patches of rust, is encrusted with ornaments of chrome and with glass reflectors of red and yellow and blue and green. All four fenders bear heavily bechromed and reflectored mudflaps. Though the car has no radio, it has a tall aerial flying an American flag half worn away in the winds of the Berlews' haste to get somewhere else.

And far be it from Lightning to save or borrow the money to buy a car in good condition; that would involve a connection and obligation that would be too permanent. Better to buy a worn-out car that is cheap enough to require no such bondage, ornament it like a carnival paradise, and then be forever replacing its worn-out parts with other worn-out parts, and work harder at night to keep it running than you work in the daytime for pay.

It comes to Mat suddenly—so that he first grimaces and then grunts—that the Berlews and the Pettits represent the two halves of the same distraction. What the Pettits are is what the Berlews dream of being. Is not the Berlews' old car the hopeless dream of a Cadillac? Is not their tireless going a persistently frustrated pilgrimage in search of Easy Street? That the Pettits *live* on Easy Street makes no essential difference between them and the Berlews. If the Pettits are what the Berlews would like to be, they are also what the Pettits would like to be; they have imagined nothing higher than they are.

And now, not out of the quiet of the evening as he hoped, but out of a fierce and defiant loyalty, Mat recovers the thought of Old Jack.

He remembers himself, a boy in college, home for the summer, recounting something lengthy and abstruse that he had learned from his books, seeking in some foolish way to impress his uncle. He sees Jack pause in his work and straighten to look at him, and then turn his back and go ahead.

"If you're going to talk to me, Mat, you'll have to walk."

He had a quality about him that Mat has always thought of as level-footed. He stood unconditionally where he stood. He was straight as a tree and stood like one, so charged with purpose and with strength that when your eye first caught him he seemed to have just risen with the sudden thrust and balance of a horse rearing. It was only with the second look that you saw that this stance was natural to him, his gift that he possessed regardlessly as he wore his clothes.

If the say-so was his, Mat knows how Old Jack would be taken to his grave. He would be taken in secret to a place at the edge of one of his fields, and only the few who loved him best would be permitted to go that far with him. They would dig a grave there and lay him in. They would say such words as might come to them, or say nothing. They would cover him and leave him there where he had belonged from birth. They would leave no stone or marker. They would level the grave with the ground. When the last of them who knew its place had died, Old Jack's return would be complete. He would be lost to memory in that field, silently possessed by the earth on which he once established the work of his hands.

But that is not to be. What is to be Mat foresaw and has been unable to prevent. And the time is at hand again, for now he hears the sound of an expensive engine in the yard.

Eleven : Here We Leave Him to His Rest

The day of Old Jack's funeral is bright. Except for Mat—who stayed at the house to visit with the Pettits, his guests overnight—the tobacco cutters worked through the morning. But now they are here, come with the dead to the grave's edge, beyond which all is dark to them.

It is not a large gathering, but at that there are too few chairs beneath the undertaker's awning over the grave. And so the women sit and most of the men stand. In the first row of chairs are Clara and Glad Pettit, Margaret Feltner, Bess Catlett, Mary Penn, and Hannah Coulter. In the second row are Mrs. Hendrick with five of her boarders. In the third and last are several neighboring wives, there more for Mat's and Margaret's sake than for Old Jack's. Mat and Burley and Jarrat and Nathan and Elton and Wheeler, who have borne the coffin to the trestle over the grave, stand under the edge of the awning, uncomfortable because in those circumstances their movements and postures seem to take on a formality that they do not intend. In another staggered row at the back of the shelter stand several other men of the town.

To Mat's surprise nothing was ever said to contradict this part of his plan. A simple graveside service is apparently what it is to be. His dealings with the Pettits during their overnight stay were polite and peaceable, if not particularly warm. Of all that he is glad enough. But now his principal emotion is the wish to be away from this that has nothing to do with Old Jack's life—or, for that matter, his death. He longs for something more fitting than this, if it is only to go home and sit by himself in the barn. Standing between Burley and Wheeler with his hands clasped behind his back, he lets his mind return, with the eagerness of a boy on holiday, to the common substances of his life. He would like to turn around and let his eyes travel over the familiar shapes of his own fields that he knows are lying in the sunlight beyond the stony horizon of the graveyard. "The fields beyond the grave," he thinks. If he were going to speak at Old Jack's funeral he would speak of them.

But now Brother Wingfare steps between his seated auditors and the grave. He turns to the Book of Psalms in the little Testament that he carries in his hand, and begins to read: "The Lord is my shepherd; I shall not want. He maketh me to lie down in green pastures: he leadeth me beside the still waters." He reads well, better than most, and Mat is moved by the reading. The preacher reads straight through the list of psalms that Mat gave him to the last of them, the one that ends: "The Lord shall preserve thy going out and thy coming in from this time forth, and even for evermore."

"Good!" Mat thinks. "Let him stop there and that will be fine."

The preacher closes the book softly, holding it on the upraised palm of his left hand; he lays the palm of his right hand gently upon the shut cover, and he raises his eyes to the canvas.

"O Lord," he says, "our gracious and merciful Heavenly Father, we are gathered here on this beautiful early autumn day to commit to thy hands the spirit and to the earth the body of our beloved father and kinsman and friend, Mr. Jack Beechum. O Lord, it is a sad and sorrowful journey that we must make to the graveside of our departed loved ones, but we know that thou hast provided comforts there to erase forever from our hearts the memory of our sufferings here."

And then Mat exercises for the first time his prerogative as the oldest man. He turns his back and gazes upon his fields.

It is a long prayer that the preacher prays. He tells the Lord that the departed loved one was not a man of the church, and seldom attended, but that in talking to his daughter he (Brother Wingfare) has found that toward the end of his life the departed showed unmistakable signs of turning toward an acceptance of Jesus Christ as his personal Savior. He speaks of what a blessed relief it is to know that all a man has to do is believe in the saving power of Jesus Christ in order to be spared the everlasting torments of Hell. He says that his hearers may therefore rest assured that the departed loved one is even at this moment sitting at the right hand of his Savior. He predicts that certain ones among his hearers may at an appropriate time also wish to accept Christ as their Savior, for clearly it is not the dead to whom we speak at these sad occasions but to the living. In a long exposition of the dynamics of grace and salvation he then bids fair to convert any doubters among those within the sound of his voice, on earth or in Heaven. He gives thanks for the general well-being of the community, for the divine favor that has been showered upon the government and the people of the United States of America, for the bountiful harvest even now in progress, and for the beautiful early autumn day. And having thus notified the Almighty of so much, the truth or error of which He presumably already knew, Brother Wingfare concludes by imploring special blessings upon the heads of the bereaved mourners in their hour of sorrow.

The preacher pockets his Testament and bends to take the hands of the Pettits. The others, by pairs and threes, detach themselves from the gathering. Quiet conversations begin. As the last word was said the men put on their hats, and now they smoke.

Clara Pettit approaches Mat now and extends her hand. "Mat, thanks for all you've done."

Mat nods. There is no reply he can make to that. What he has done he has done for Old Jack's sake, or his own sake, not for hers. And much that he intended has been undone. He and Clara owe each other nothing. But he smiles. He pats her hand. "Well," he says, "it was good to see you in these parts again."

She gives his hand a parting squeeze and moves on to speak to Margaret. Standing up the slope between the grave and their car, Glad is waiting for her, anxious to be gone, the hearse having already departed. Catching Mat's eye, Glad gives him a quick grin and wave of farewell. Mat nods.

Clara comes up to Glad and he takes her arm. They turn and start up toward their car, picking their way among the stones. Now that Old Jack is dead and Clara has seen him borne to the grave in a style fitting to her taste, she is free of this place. She has put the past behind her. She is already thirty years gone. In her high heels she walks uncertainly on the deep sod, as though wading, but with determined haste. She does not look at the ground. Walking on it, she asserts her difference from it.

For the moment oblivious to all else, Mat watches her. She and Glad get into the car and start it and move off down the drive. As they reach the gate and turn into the road, though even now they do not look back, Mat waves.

He stands facing the road. Behind him the footsteps and voices have begun to move off up the slope. He knows that Margaret is standing behind him, waiting for him. But for some time still Mat does not move. He stands like another of the inscribed stones, bearing the graved name of what is gone.

Twelve: Wheeler

In the warm clear sunlight pouring upon the ridges and slopes and woods and roofs and walls, the brushy fence rows, pastures, cornfields, and dwindling tobacco patches of that country as deeply familiar to him as if both dreamed and seen, Wheeler Catlett drives his car out the Birds Branch Road. He drives slowly up the rises and then lets the car drift down again of its own weight. On the steering wheel his fingers beat a light, gentle, unattended rhythm while he watches the country open ahead of him and go by. He left Bess at the Feltners' after the funeral, saying that he had an errand to do before they went home. But it is not just the errand. Wheeler Catlett has thinking to do. Like Mat and the others, he has recognized Old Jack's death as one of the crucial divisions in his own life. And he has felt a need, as yet obscure to him, to let his mind and his eyes drift a while again upon the country, to sense himself again as native and belonging there, and perhaps at last to feel established in his life whatever change it is that has been made.

For nearly thirty years Wheeler has been involved in the founding and the administration and the defense of a marketing cooperative whose purpose is to assure a decent living, a chance to survive on their land, to the farmers of this part of the country. It is a Jeffersonian vision, one might say, that the cooperative was founded to implement and preserve, but in Wheeler the effort was founded also upon an impulse sterner and more personal: as a boy he had seen his father and his neighbors sell their crops for too little to pay the warehouse commission; he had seen the time when the market was a tragedy in which good men saw their ruin. With a child's clear sense of justice he determined then to do something about it if he could. And in considerable measure he and his friends in the cooperative have so far succeeded in doing something about it. But the complexity of Wheeler's history has been that in order to serve and defend the way of life that he loves and respects above all others, he has had to leave it to live another kind of life, first in college and law school and then in the courthouse town of Hargrave.

And yet he has stayed near enough to home—to the farms and households and sickbeds and then the graves of those men whose worthiness and whose troubles first defined his aims—so that he has always had clearly in mind what it was he served. Now Old Jack, who was the last of that generation that Wheeler looked to with such filial devotion, is dead. And Wheeler is fifty-two years old, as old as the century, and younger men are looking to him. Now he must cease to be a son to the old men and become a father to the young. He has his own sons, of course. But there are also the young men of the farms, coming on, men such as Elton Penn and Nathan Coulter, in whom the old way has survived. Wheeler has been thinking about them and about the troubles that probably lie ahead of them: an increasing scarcity of labor as more and more of the country people move to the cities; the consequent necessity for further mechanization of the farms; the consequent need of the farmers for more land and more capital in order to survive; the consequent further departure of the labor force from the country; the increasing difficulty of preserving an agricultural economy favorable to small farmers as political power flows from the country to the cities. These interlinking chains of consequence have lain heavily upon Wheeler's mind for years. But Old Jack's death has raised anew and more starkly than ever the possibility that men of his kind are a race doomed to extinction, that the men Wheeler loves most in the world are last survivors. Driving out the Birds Branch Road this afternoon, he sees the farms and their fences and fields and buildings as never before in the light and shadow of a human history that had its beginning in time, and will have its end. His eyes lingering familiarly over the lay of the fields in the brilliant fall sunlight, he muses upon the mortality not of individual men and women but of the human life of the earth.

As the white buildings of Old Jack's place become visible among the shade trees at the top of the rise, Wheeler drives even more slowly, and his eyes move more carefully still over the ground. Year by year, for almost as long as Wheeler has been conscious of it, the place has been improved by Jack Beechum's impassioned kindness to it. Even after Old Jack's departure his kindness remained, and then Elton and Wheeler himself were its agents; between them they made the plans and did the work to carry out the old man's wishes. During the war years and afterwards the farm made money. And Old Jack—whose own wants and needs, never great, had become small indeed—turned his earnings to further improvements on the farm. Elton was eager to do the work and to see it done, and incited and pleased by that eagerness in the young man, Old Jack spared no expense. It has become a place a man like Wheeler would drive or walk many miles to admire.

He turns in at the gate and drives slowly up through the yard under the limbs of the old trees, and past the house and into the barn lot. He stops the car in front of the barn and gets out. He steps through the wide doorway into the hay-fragrant shadow, nearly blinding after the bright sun. He calls quietly: "Elton?"

Getting no answer, he turns and stands looking thoughtfully out across the lot. The Penns' automobile is parked on the grass near the back porch. They cannot be long home from the funeral. Elton is probably still at the house, changing his clothes.

Though he is alone, Wheeler has about him an air of alertness, of implicit haste; he seems to be not resting but poised in passage. It was this quality perhaps more than any other that endeared him to Old Jack. Wheeler could get things done, and Old Jack liked that.

Now, seeing Elton come out of the house, Wheeler steps forward into the light of the doorway. Elton has changed from the suit he wore to the funeral back into his work clothes.

"Hello, Wheeler," Elton says, stepping into the barn. "It's a pretty day, ain't it?"

But now that he has spoken of it, his satisfaction with the weather seems to him unfitting. He turns and stands beside Wheeler, like him looking out into the daylight for a good many seconds before either of them speaks again. It is as though they are two of an assembly of spectators, and this passage of the light is an event they will be long and quiet in watching.

And then Wheeler says: "It is. It's a fine day."

For a while again they are silent. There is an embarrassment between them that neither of them expected or prepared for. It is only now that it exists that they realize its possibility. Until now their two lives have been bound together by their mutual allegiance to a third life, Old Jack's. They wait to see what they may mean to each other now.

Wheeler feels the abruptness of the first words that he must speak beyond Old Jack's death and the change it has made: "Elton, Uncle Jack arranged in his will for you to buy this place. He set the price and left you half the cost."

Elton looks at Wheeler quickly, a peculiar challenge in his eyes.

"He'll begin to believe it about day after tomorrow," Wheeler thinks. He grins at Elton and says: "He didn't want to leave it to you outright. He thought you ought to work for it the way he did. It was his opinion, you know, that there were some essential things he never learned until he got in debt." Wheeler laughs briefly, and then, as if to keep his mind strictly on its business, looks at the ground. "I was to tell you as soon as he was buried and not wait, so you could make your plans."

There is another silence of some length, and then Elton says: "Well, Wheeler, I reckon the old boss has got a little too far away to thank."

"He thought you were worthy," Wheeler says. "You were a son to him."

He hears Elton draw a long, careful breath, and after a moment draw another.

"I was going to work some of my tobacco ground this afternoon, Wheeler, while we're not cutting. I reckon I'd better go do it. I thank you."

"Sure," Wheeler says. "I've got to be going myself. We'll be talking."

But he does not move. He stands still, listening, as Elton's footsteps go around the barn. He hears the tractor engine start and move out the ridge. And then instead of getting into his car, Wheeler walks slowly up and down the driveway of the barn, the sense of change, of loss, of the passing of things suddenly heavy upon him. For years he has come here as Old Jack's friend and agent and emissary, almost as his son. Now that is over, but he cannot yet bring himself to leave. It is as though he has carried and passed on some key, some vital power, from an old man to a young one, and he thinks of the distance he has come.

He walks the length of the driveway three times, at a loss, filled with an objectless grief, and then on an impulse opens the door of what used to be the harness room and steps inside. At first he sees nothing that he might have come looking for. The room is dim and orderly—a bin of feed, three empty barrels, hand tools, buckets, all placed neatly and handily around the walls, the floor swept, several old sets of harness hanging on pegs—but its present order supersedes by several years any order that Old Jack ever made.

Only after his eyes grow used to the dimness does Wheeler begin to see, hanging against the walls above shoulder level, the evidence of Old Jack's time. Hanging from nails driven everywhere into the boards are various pieces of harness, collars, collar pads, an odd hame, a set of check lines, pieces of leather strap, short lengths of rope, iron rings, snaps, lengths of chain, the iron fittings for singletrees and doubletrees, a wooden pulley, lap rings, clevises, plow plates, rusty horse and mule shoes, bridle bits, a broken shovel handle—the leftovers and odds and ends of a lifetime of farming, too good to throw away.

In the days before Old Jack moved to town, Wheeler remembers, when one of his tenants would ask where something was, the old man would answer indignantly: *"Hanging up!"*

Of course it was hanging up! He had been hanging things up all his life, taking care of things, keeping his leavings out from under his feet. If what he picked up had no place, he drove a new nail and made one.

"Hanging up!" he would say, to the bewilderment and intimidation of whoever dared ask, for though he grew ever less likely to remember where he had hung it, he knew there was no need to look for it underfoot.

Among that assortment of possibly useful objects that Old Jack saved and hung up, Wheeler comes upon a 1936 campaign poster of Franklin Roosevelt, bearing in black capitals the legend: A GALLANT LEADER. Wheeler himself was county chairman for that campaign, and he must have given the poster to Old Jack, who admired Roosevelt mainly for the game look of him in his pictures and for his willingness to place himself in difficulty. The paper is badly worn, torn, creased, snagged, brown at the edges. All the white area of the paper is covered with figures and with writing in Old Jack's hand, whose laborious engraving Wheeler had observed a thousand times. ("You don't have to push it clean through the paper," he would say. "Damn it, son," Old Jack would say, "*I been to school!*") At the top of the poster, above the legend, is written: "Gray mare bred May 10" and near the bottom, at a slant, in blacker pencil: "spotted sow to Ware Clayborn's boar March 17" and under that, at a slightly different slant: "10 pigs lost 2."

There are several more dates without explanation, and the rest of the space is filled with figures, additions and subtractions as abstract and unmeaning now as a child's exercises in arithmetic. But though the writings on it have shed whatever significance they may have had, to Wheeler, who knows something of the solitude and the passion and at times the desperation of that account-keeping, the scribbled poster appears as a sort of emblem of Old Jack. Now that he looks, the whole wall is covered with those dates and figures that when they were written were never just figures, but the visible tracks of Jack Beechum's mind, planning and counting, saying what was lost, what was left.

Wheeler remembers the successor to that wall, the little notebook that Old Jack carried in the bib of his overalls during his life at the hotel, and all the fierce and sporting arguments it led to. He laughs. And then, without realizing that he is about to do it, he cries.

Standing there has become pointless, pointlessly painful. Making up his mind to go, he carefully takes the old poster loose from the wall. He intends, as he removes the nails, to make a keepsake of it. But once he has taken it down and is holding it in his hands, its meaning seems already to have diminished. In a kind of guilt, in the sort of haste with which one would stop the bleeding of a living thing, he nails it back where it was.

"No," he thinks, "we'll take no trophies, no souvenirs. Let it fall like a leaf."

Epilogue

In mid-December of the year of Old Jack's death they are all in the stripping room on the place soon to be known as Elton Penn's: Mat Feltner, the Coulter brothers and Nathan, Elton, Andy Catlett, home from the university for the holidays, and his brother Henry. All that cloudy, cold day they have been working in the heavy scent of the cured tobacco, the wind heaving and sucking at the room's little cell of warmth, the drizzle brushing the tin roof in fits. When night comes it will freeze and snow.

They have stood all day at the bench under the light of the row of north windows, each man stripping his grade from the stalks and passing them on, tying the leaves into hands, straddling the bound hands onto sticks, carrying the filled sticks to the presses. They have carried in great armloads of tobacco from the covered bulk in the barn, and have carried bundles of stripped stalks through the door at the opposite end of the room to a pile outside. They have speculated extravagantly upon Andy's behavior at college and upon his prospects. They have teased both boys about their love life. They have anticipated first dinner and then supper. In the way of old comradeship they have spoken of what they know and remember in common; they have said much that they have said before. And now for some time they have said nothing. Their long standing at their work has put the ache of weariness in their backs and shoulders, and they are waiting for the day to end. Out the windows the light has already begun to deaden. It will not be long.

They hear an automobile pull up in the front of the barn and stop. Its door opens and shuts. Presently Wheeler Catlett steps into the room, dressed for the office. His day finished there, he drove up to see to things on his farm, and now has come here to visit a while in the warmth and to get his boys. He stands with his back to the stove, his hands opened behind him to its heat, while the others go on working at the bench.

Now, except for Old Jack himself, they are all here. There comes a brief gust of talk about the market and the weather, as if only to include Wheeler in the silence that follows, in which they hear again the wind, the hardening drizzle, the crackling in the stove.

Going to one of the presses, Elton removes a stick of bound bright leaves as long as a man's arm and holds it to the light.

"How about that, Wheeler? Wouldn't the old boss have loved to see that?"

Burley Coulter laughs and gives the well-remembered response: "By God, son, you're a good one! You're all right! You've got a good head on your shoulders, and you'll do!"

And now, as though he is with them again, in the old uproar of his commendation and censure his words pass among them, possessing their tongues.

"Son, do you owe anybody anything? Well, you won't amount to a damn until you do."

"I know what a man can do in a day."

"If you're going to talk to me, you'll have to walk."

"Ready *hell!* I *been* ready!"

"Out of my head, by God, that knew this business before you were born, and had a hat on it three hours before you were out of bed."

"While there's light to see by, they'd better have their eyes open."

"Settle for the half-assed, and then, by God, *admire* it!"

"Hanging up!"

"Where are you, son? Damn it to hell. It's *daylight!*"

In all their minds his voice lies beneath a silence. And in the hush of it they are aware of something that passed from them and now returns: his stubborn biding with them to the end, his keeping of faith with them who would live after him, and what perhaps none of them has yet thought to call his gentleness, his long gentleness toward them and toward this place where they are at work. They know that his memory holds them in common knowledge and common loss. The like of him will not soon live again in this world, and they will not forget him.

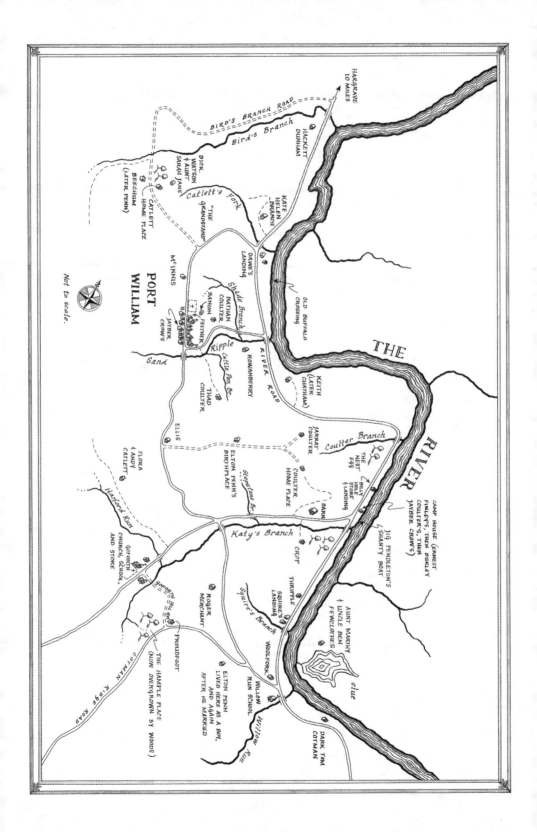

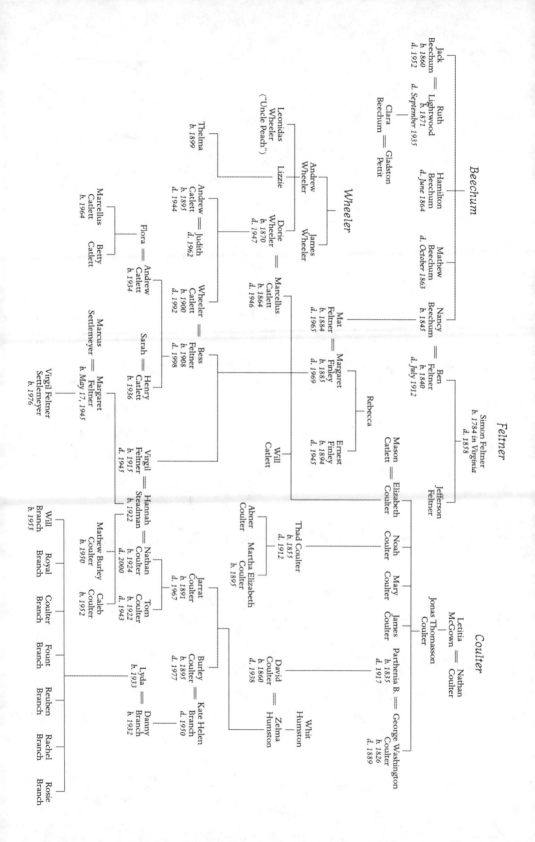